ALSO BY SHARON M. DRAPER

November Blues
Copper Sun
Romiette and Julio
We Beat the Street: How a Friendship Pact Led to Success
The Battle of Jericho
Double Dutch

HAZELWOOD HIGH TRILOGY
Tears of a Tiger
Forged by Fire
Darkness Before Dawn

ZIGGY AND THE BLACK DINOSAURS SERIES
The Buried Bones Mystery
Lost in the Tunnel of Time
Shadows of Caesar's Creek
The Space Mission Adventure
The Backyard Animal Show
Stars and Sparks Onstage

FIRE FROM THE ROCK

FIRE
FROM THE
ROCK

SHARON M. DRAPER

Dutton Children's Books

DUTTON CHILDREN'S BOOKS
A division of Penguin Young Readers Group

Published by the Penguin Group
Penguin Group (USA) Inc., 375 Hudson Street, New York, New York 10014, U.S.A. | Penguin
Group (Canada), 90 Eglinton Avenue East, Suite 700, Toronto, Ontario, Canada M4P 2Y3 (a division
of Pearson Penguin Canada Inc.) | Penguin Books Ltd, 80 Strand, London WC2R 0RL, England
| Penguin Ireland, 25 St Stephen's Green, Dublin 2, Ireland (a division of Penguin Books Ltd) |
Penguin Group (Australia), 250 Camberwell Road, Camberwell, Victoria 3124, Australia (a division of
Pearson Australia Group Pty Ltd) | Penguin Books India Pvt Ltd, 11 Community Centre, Panchsheel
Park, New Delhi - 110 017, India | Penguin Group (NZ), 67 Apollo Drive, Rosedale, North Shore
0745, Auckland, New Zealand (a division of Pearson New Zealand Ltd) | Penguin Books (South
Africa) (Pty) Ltd, 24 Sturdee Avenue, Rosebank, Johannesburg 2196, South Africa | Penguin Books
Ltd, Registered Offices: 80 Strand, London WC2R 0RL, England

CIP Data is available.

Published in the United States by Dutton Children's Books,
a division of Penguin Young Readers Group
345 Hudson Street, New York, New York 10014
www.penguin.com/youngreaders

DESIGNED BY IRENE VANDERVOORT

Printed in USA   First Edition

1 3 5 7 9 10 8 6 4 2

ISBN 978-0-525-47720-4

FIRE FROM THE ROCK

LITTLE ROCK, ARKANSAS
1957

*"Fire came up from the rock
and consumed the meat and the bread."*
JUDGES 6:21

*"Is not My word like fire and
like a hammer that smashes rock?"*
JEREMIAH 23:29

Help! Mama, come quick! Donna Jean's been bit by a dog!" fifteen-year-old Sylvia Patterson screamed as she burst through the front door. Her hat had fallen off, she'd lost a snow boot someplace back on the sidewalk, and her breath escaped in short, harsh gasps. Sylvia had never been so scared in her life.

Her aunt Bessie hurried up the steps behind her, struggling with the weight of the sobbing, shrieking eight-year-old in her arms. She paused on the porch to adjust the child's weight and to try to quiet her a bit.

"*Sh-sh-sh*, child. It's gonna be all right. Your mama's gonna make it all better real soon. We're at your house now. That's a girl. Be brave now. *Sh-sh-sh*."

Donna Jean's tears turned into big gulps as she realized she was home, but as soon as she saw her mother running to the door, she started wailing again.

"Oh, my Lord! How did this happen?" The girls' mother looked upset, but her movements were surprisingly calm. She took the little girl into her arms and cuddled her as she rushed the child into the house and set her gently on the sofa. Rust-colored blood had stained her apron.

"It was one of Mr. Crandall's big old hound dogs, Mama! He came out of nowhere and just grabbed her leg!" Sylvia cried.

"Run go get me some soap and water, towels from the bathroom, some rubbing alcohol, a bottle of iodine, and the box of gauze strips, Sylvie," her mother said calmly. Sylvia darted off quickly to obey, partly from fear, and partly from not wanting to miss one second of this horrible drama that was unfolding in her living room. When she dashed back her mother was cooing to the little girl, "It's all right, baby. It's just a little scratch," but her forehead had wrinkled into a frown as she examined Donna Jean's leg.

"How did this happen, Bessie?" Mrs. Patterson asked her sister.

Aunt Bessie sighed deeply as she took the alcohol and bandages from the still-trembling Sylvia. "I feel like it's my fault, Leola, but how was I to know that Crandall's fool dogs were loose? The girls were just waiting for me by the fence, and the dog tore around the corner like a train off the track. He wrapped his jaws around her leg before I could turn around. Oh, Lord." She put her head in her hands.

Every colored person in Little Rock, Arkansas, knew all about the Crandall family and their vicious dogs. Mr. Crandall—the owner of a local barbershop, and surely the meanest man in the county—had trained his dogs to attack Negroes. Sometimes he conveniently forgot to tie them up. All his friends probably thought it was really funny, but all the colored people thought it was terrifying. Last year at least five people—all of them Negroes—had been bitten by one of his dogs.

Crandall's wife, Eileen, was known as the most vocal segregationist in town. She and her friends—all of whom wore cat-eye-shaped glasses, Sylvia had noticed—protested vocally when the buses, the police force, and the university had been integrated. They had recently formed something called The Mothers' Coalition to prepare for protesting against possible school integration.

The Crandalls had two teenaged children—a thick-shouldered, crew-cut-wearing son named Johnny, who was an outstanding player on the Central High football team, and a thin, pale daughter named Callie, who mirrored her mother in looks and attitude.

Sylvia and the rest of her friends walked to school the long way rather than go past the Crandalls' house. *Aunt Bessie should have known better!* Sylvia thought angrily. She bit her lip, frustrated with herself as well. *I should have known better, too.*

With its peeling yellow paint and the sagging front porch, the Crandall house looked dingy, but Mr. Crandall made it just plain frightening. His hair was greased back, and his eyes, even at a distance, looked dark and fierce. The local children whispered that he could cast spells with those eyes.

Even though Mr. Crandall seemed to wear the same pair of work pants every day, he was known throughout Little Rock for his highly polished, chestnut-brown, double-laced oxford shoes with metal taps on the toes and the heels. Folks said he special-ordered those shoes from Houston, Texas. In addition, he made a point of wearing a clean white dress shirt every day. His wife never ironed them, however. He always hired women like Aunt Bessie to do his shirts. Today she had taken twenty-five bright-white dress shirts to him, bleached and starched so well they looked like little soldiers.

Sylvia watched quietly while her mother worked on her sister, not sure if she should cry or throw up. She took deep breaths of the stuffy air in the living room, but she felt dizzy and enclosed.

"I just went to deliver his laundry," Aunt Bessie said, weeping, as she helped her sister wash Donna Jean's wounds.

Some of the water in the basin, tinged pink with DJ's blood, sloshed onto the carpet as DJ's mother squeezed out the washcloth.

"Why are you still doing laundry, anyway?" Sylvia's mother asked angrily. "You've got a successful beauty shop. You don't need to be doing this!"

Bessie nodded her head in agreement. "I know, I know. I shouldn't have taken the girls with me, but I'd promised them a treat—you know how much they love Mrs. Zucker's cookies." Donna Jean had stopped screaming and only cried out when they touched a particularly tender area.

"You know, you're the only colored woman in Little Rock who will still do laundry for that fool," her sister said bitterly. "You let him talk to you like you're a child, and he only pays you ten cents a shirt."

Sylvia looked up in surprise. Her mother rarely showed anger against anyone, especially her own sister.

"You used to work for his wife," Aunt Bessie retorted.

"I went one time. Then, because she treated me like dirt, I refused to go back, like you should have years ago," her mother said flatly.

Aunt Bessie's shoulders drooped. She had told the girls to wait for her outside Mr. Crandall's back fence while she collected her two dollars and fifty cents. Mr. Crandall always took a long time because he checked every shirt for brown marks or water spots before he would pay her.

Hateful old man never finds any spots—he just likes to make Aunt Bessie stand there in the cold. Sylvia noticed her hands were squeezed into fists.

"It was cold, Mama," Sylvia explained quietly. "Donna Jean had the jump rope she got for Christmas and she was jumping a little to keep warm, I guess. Both of us were giggling and acting silly—maybe a little scared, too. Then that dog got loose and headed straight for Donna Jean. I tried to get her out of the way, Mama—really I did—but the dog was too fast."

Sylvia kept replaying the scene in her mind, trying to figure out how she could have been faster, quicker, smarter—something that might have helped her sister. *But superheroes only exist in my comic books,* Sylvia thought with a sigh. *In real life innocent children bleed and people like me just feel guilty and helpless.*

Her mother reached over and gave Sylvia a hug. "It's not your fault, child," she said gently. "You did the best you could. Donna Jean is going to be just fine."

Sylvia pulled away. "But it shouldn't have happened, Mama! What kind of person trains a dog to bite little children?" she asked angrily.

"A hateful man is an unhappy man," her mother replied philosophically.

"Well, I hope he chokes on his misery!" Sylvia paced around the small living room, not able to channel her anger.

Donna Jean whimpered softly. "It hurts, Mama."

"I know, baby. Mama's gonna fix it. Lie still now, you hear?"

"Should we take her to the hospital?" Sylvia asked, her voice tight.

"The wounds aren't deep. As long as we don't let them get infected, I think she'll be all right," her mother responded. She was bathing Donna Jean's leg with alcohol, daubing it with iodine, and wrapping it with clean, white gauze. Sylvia felt a little dizzy because the red iodine made the wound look even bloodier than it really was.

Aunt Bessie continued. "I dropped the shirts onto the porch and ran screaming toward Donna Jean with a shirt hanger in my hand. I beat that dog off her."

"Mr. Crandall really started cursing then, Mama," Sylvia explained. "He told Aunt Bessie that she would have to do every single one of those shirts over again, plus pay for any injuries to his dog. Can you believe that?"

"He can let that dog wash and iron his shirts!" Aunt Bessie said angrily. "Never again, Leola. Never again!"

"Or his lazy, busybody wife," Sylvia's mother mumbled, almost to herself.

Sylvia couldn't help smiling at the thought of a huge, snarling hound dog standing in front of an ironing board, calmly pressing shirts. Then the memory of the real dog, teeth bared, its eyes red with rage, sobered her.

She told her mother, "When Mr. Crandall finally came over to tie up the dog, he said to us, 'Stupid gal ought not to rile up good hunting dogs.'"

"I believe he was smiling when he said it, Leola," Aunt Bessie said. "He and his drinking buddies will have a good laugh about this tonight."

Mrs. Patterson's face showed a mixture of sorrow and bitterness, but she made no comment because just then Gary burst through the front door. A cold wind always seemed to follow him, Sylvia thought with a shudder, even when the weather was warm. At seventeen, her brother was tall and thin, with large, slightly crooked teeth, and he wore his hair straightened and slicked back in the style many of the teenaged boys thought made them look good. He took one glance at Donna Jean, the blood, the bandages, and the look of defeat on his mother's face, and he cried out, "What's going on? Who hurt my baby sister?" He clenched his fists. He wore his anger like clothing.

"She's fine, Gary," his mother said, trying to calm him with her voice. "She had an unfortunate run-in with a dog."

"One of Crandall's dogs attacked her?" Gary looked around wildly, then, in one swift movement, grabbed the poker from the fireplace.

"It was an accident, Gary. The dog got loose, and Donna Jean got in the way. There's nothing we can do," his mother said, her voice pleading now.

"He has trained those dogs to attack us!" Gary cried. "I'll kill it! I swear I'll kill all those vicious beasts!" Sylvia looked terrified as Gary's anger seemed to dart about the room looking for ways to escape.

Aunt Bessie grabbed his upraised arm and took the poker from him. "No, you won't, Gary. Calm down. You'll only bring trouble to this family. Just leave well enough alone. Your sister is not seriously injured. Let it be for now."

Gary retorted, "No, I can't just let it be. Crandall needs to be punished! How can you *live* like this—never taking a stand, always letting them hurt you?"

"The Bible says vengeance belongs to the Lord," his mother replied quietly.

Gary shook his head in disbelief. "What about you, Sylvia?" Gary asked. "Are you going to stay in the Amen Corner with the old folks, or open your eyes and look at the future?"

Sylvia blinked, unsure what to say. She remembered her brother as a freckle-faced boy who loved to climb trees, who insisted on going to the very top where the branches got thin and he swayed in the wind. To Sylvia he used to be better than Batman when it came to beating up her imaginary monsters. But this was very real and very scary. "I just want things to be like they used to be," Sylvia said helplessly, "when we were little and nothing bad could hurt us."

"You're going to have to get over that and move on," Gary said harshly. He ignored the hurt look on Sylvia's face. He walked over to the sofa then, knelt down, and said gently to his youngest sister, "It won't always be like this, DJ, but I will always protect you, understand?" She looked up at him solemnly and nodded. He kissed her on the cheek, then walked back out of the door, saying nothing more to the rest of them. The door slammed loudly.

Sylvia trembled a little as swirls of his fury seemed to settle on the carpet. They finished tending to Donna Jean without speaking. Finally, when the child was all bandaged, had been given an aspirin and some hot tea to drink, they tucked her in with a warm blanket and she finally fell asleep.

Sylvia's mother and aunt moved to the kitchen table, sipping the cinnamon tea that Sylvia had made for them. Sylvia poured a cup for herself, hoping they would invite her to join them. She was pleased when they nodded in her direction.

"I worry about Gary," Sylvia's mother said as she sipped

her tea. "He is angry and impetuous at a time when we need to be patient. The Bible says blessings come to those who wait."

Sylvia felt like groaning, but she didn't. She was sick of her mother's Bible verses and platitudes, but she knew better than to say anything.

"We've been waiting a long time, Leola," Aunt Bessie said. "Maybe the young folks have a point."

Sylvia wished her mother would be more understanding of Gary's need to fix the world in a hurry. As far as she could tell, not much had been accomplished in Little Rock by waiting.

Sylvia's mother ignored her sister and said, "And Lester is going be really upset that his baby girl got hurt."

"Hmmph! Angry enough to confront old Crandall?" Aunt Bessie asked as she flashed her eyes. "I doubt it. Probably just pray himself into a corner like he usually does."

Mrs. Patterson got up, walked over to the sink, and began to scrub her favorite iron skillet. Sylvia knew that anytime her mother got angry or upset, she'd start to clean something— dishes, rugs, walls—anything to channel her emotions. "Lester is a good man. Don't belittle his beliefs," Mrs. Patterson replied sharply. "If we don't depend on our faith, haven't we sunk to the level of people like Crandall?"

"That whole pack of dogs he keeps ought to be shot!" Aunt Bessie said angrily. "I'm getting tired of feeling helpless all the time, and praying just isn't enough anymore!"

"Are we going to call the police?" Sylvia asked, finally speaking up. She ached to see Mr. Crandall punished, but she didn't look directly at her aunt or her mother as she sipped her tea.

"We'll let your father decide when he gets home," her

mother replied, "but I doubt it. They won't do anything to Crandall, and Donna Jean is going to recuperate."

"So he's just going to get *away* with this?" Sylvia almost choked on her tea. "Maybe Gary is right! It's been almost a hundred years since slavery was over. This is 1957 and we shouldn't have to put up with treatment like this!" Sylvia couldn't believe she was raising her voice to her mother, and even more, that her mother was letting her do so.

"They will say it was an accident, Sylvie. Just a case of a dog protecting its property. We have to save our calls to the police for real life-threatening events."

"I don't get it!" Sylvia cried out to her mother and her aunt. When she thought about her little sister lying there with her leg wrapped up, she understood how Gary wanted to fight rather than pray.

Her mother didn't respond, only continued to scrub pots that already gleamed, and Aunt Bessie finished her tea. The kitchen was silent.

Finally Aunt Bessie began to hum an old spiritual that Sylvia heard every Sunday at church. Sylvia's mother joined her gradually, her alto voice low and full of sorrow. Sylvia, feeling unsettled and confused, sat there quietly, picking at the pattern in the tablecloth, listening to their voices drift up like soft smoke.

Wednesday, January 2, 1957

I love my new diary. Mama seems to know what I need even before I ask. When I looked in my stocking on Christmas morning, there it was—a pale green, leather-looking, golden-trimmed little book with a tiny lock and key.

The pages are thin—all clean and smooth with little blue lines just waiting for me. I had planned to fill the first page with lovely words and ideas, but instead I'm forced to write about that dog, that blood, my sister's screams. I hate old Crandall! Is that a sin? I'm sure Daddy would say so. I don't care. Crandall needs to be put in a pen full of vicious snakes with poison fangs or something horrible like that—maybe even wolves or tigers or hyenas—and left there overnight! But maybe not. When I really think about it, it's not hatred I feel, but hurt. Why do people have to be so mean?

I don't know how adults deal with stuff like this every day. Mama is very proper, which gets her in trouble with white folks sometimes. They say she's "putting on airs," but she's really just being herself. She won't go out of the house without her white gloves and a black straw hat. When we take the bus downtown to shop, she makes me wear my white gloves, too, even though for the life of me I cannot figure out why we need gloves in the middle of summer. But she says if you think of yourself as a lady, then no matter how the world treats you, you will always know that you are a lady inside. Mr. Crandall's dog didn't care whether Donna Jean was a lady or not. It just saw a little colored girl and jumped on her, the way it had been trained to do. White gloves and thinking like a lady would not have helped.

Even Daddy doesn't get much respect. He's so smart he could quote the whole Bible, and his sermons get everyone in church rocking, but nothing outside the church ever changes. White folks like the Crandalls don't care how hard we pray or how loud we scream hallelujah. They still hate us.

I need more than hot, sweaty emotion. It's time for something real to happen.

Mama, do I have to wear that new dress to school?" Sylvia asked at breakfast. "Why can't I wear something really neat, like a poodle skirt? I am *so* tired of being in junior high!" Sylvia was anxious to get to Horace Mann High School, where she hoped everybody would stop treating her like a kid.

"Youth is a treasure that's wasted on the young," Sylvia's mother said absentmindedly.

Sylvia sighed with exasperation.

"Who're you trying to impress, Sylvie?" Gary teased. "I've seen Reggie Birmingham looking at you at church like you were a hot roast beef sandwich!"

Sylvia smiled and blushed. "Like you look at Anita Carver?" It was Gary's turn to smile. "I dress to please myself!" Sylvia replied with as much dignity as she could.

She could tell she wasn't fooling her brother, and she really did look forward to seeing Reggie again. Since she saw him almost every Sunday at church, and every day at school since kindergarten, she'd never even considered him as a member of the opposite sex. He used to be just Reggie—as inconsequential as a bug. But somehow this year things had changed. Reggie had muscles, and a faint shadow of mustache, and eyes the color of maple syrup—things Sylvia had never noticed before.

"Anita is the only thing in Little Rock that makes me feel special. She makes me feel like a man," Gary said quietly.

"I really don't think you need one of those silly skirts, Sylvia," Mrs. Patterson told her, ignoring Gary's reference to both Anita and Reggie. "Somehow the girls who wear them just seem a little, well, fast. You know what I mean? You know what the Bible says about loose women."

"No, Mama, I don't. Rachel Zucker has three poodle skirts, and you don't think she's fast or loose, do you?"

"Rachel doesn't live under my roof, and I don't sew her clothes," Mrs. Patterson replied sharply.

Sylvia started to retort, but she thought better of it when she caught Gary's eye.

"Don't bring white folks into our kitchen," he hissed at her, low enough to be out of their parents' earshot.

Sylvia gave him a dirty look, but said nothing.

Mrs. Patterson had made fresh blueberry pancakes and the family was finishing up its long, delicious Christmas holiday of the last two weeks—filled with homemade cookies, cakes, pies, and tons of Mama-made fried chicken. Sylvia's father slurped his coffee, nibbled on the crisp, pan-fried bacon, and read a copy of the morning paper, mildly unaware of normal breakfast chatter.

Gary was unusually talkative and cheerful. No one had asked where he had gone when he stormed out of the house on Tuesday, and he had volunteered no information.

"My leg feels better," Donna Jean said as she licked the blueberry syrup off her fingers. "Will I be going to school? I don't want to get behind in my classes."

"How far behind can a kid get in third grade?" Gary teased. "What do you learn when you're eight, DJ—how to count on your fingers?"

Donna Jean grinned at him and tossed a spoon at his head. He caught it in midair and then balanced it on his nose, making her laugh.

"We'll see, little one," her mother replied. "I want to make sure none of your wounds gets infected, and I suppose we just have to hope that awful dog has no disease." Just talking about Donna Jean's injuries made her get up and start sweeping the floor, Sylvia noticed.

"Hey, Gary," Sylvia asked her brother, "would you take me to one of Mann's basketball games this season?' Horace Mann had a terrific team, and Reggie's older brother, Greg, was their top scorer. And somehow, now that she was older, the thought of watching sweaty boys run across a shiny gym floor made Sylvia's heart beat a little faster. She covered her smile, knowing her mother would never understand.

"I wanna go, too!" Donna Jean piped up.

"You'll have time enough for such," her mother said. "Finish your breakfast." Donna Jean poked out her lip.

"Maybe I'll let you come," Gary told Sylvia. "If I don't have a date. You going for the basketball, or the boys?" He grinned at her.

"Your mind stays in the gutter, boy. I'm thinking of trying out for cheerleader when I get to Mann, and I want to watch their moves. So there!" Sylvia grabbed the last piece of bacon off his plate and gobbled it.

"I'm gonna get you for that, Sylvie. Just wait until you get to school and open your lunchbox. Instead of a big fat slice of Mama's apple pie, all you'll find is a big old rock. I'll be eating your pie while I watch the cheerleaders practice!" He laughed good-naturedly. It gave the kitchen a soft, relaxed feeling.

"High school must be so much fun," Sylvia said wistfully as she imagined hanging with kids at the corner drugstore, listening to records, and going to dances and games and parties.

"Yeah, if you like coffee-breathed, homework-giving teachers who wear pearls and smell like Cashmere Bouquet dusting powder," Gary said, breaking her reverie. He poured way too much syrup on his pancakes.

"Even the men teachers?" Donna Jean asked, laughing.

"Speaking of school," Gary said to his parents, "you know there's been talk about integration." His sentence hovered above the kitchen table, threatening to ruin the pleasant morning.

"Nonsense, boy," his father mumbled. "That's going to take years to happen." He continued to read the paper, but Sylvia could tell he was no longer concentrating.

"Maybe not," Gary kept on. "Some folks say they might try to integrate Central High School by this September. And I think it's way past time," he added. Gary was good at pushing his father just over the edge.

"Don't rile your father, Gary," their mother warned. "Would you like some more eggs?"

Gary didn't look at her. His eyes were intent on his father's face. "Dad, listen. When they make a list of Negro kids who get to go to Central High, I want to be on it," he announced. The kitchen was silent except for the bubbling of the coffee in the percolator.

Their father almost choked on his bacon. "Why would you want to do a fool thing like that?" he asked. He looked at Gary as if he had grown a second skull.

"Because I deserve to go to a big, modern school, and have new books and desks and the best education in Arkansas," Gary retorted.

"It was good enough for me when I was your age," his father said, his voice tight. "We had strong Negro teachers who taught us pride in our heritage, our history, and our culture. No white school will ever do that for you."

"That was a long time ago, Dad. Things have changed." Frustration marked Gary's face. "Is it wrong to want more?"

"Maybe not wrong, but certainly dangerous," Mrs. Patterson told her son. Her voice was laced with fear. "'Danger lurks in the heart of the evildoer,'" she muttered.

Sylvia rolled her eyes at her mother's quote. She wasn't sure she should speak up, but she figured things couldn't get much worse. "Maybe Gary is right," Sylvia said quietly.

Both parents jerked their heads to look at Sylvia in amazement. "You keep out of this, young lady," her father told her.

Sylvia took a deep breath. "But, Daddy, even though Negro schools might be better, shouldn't colored kids have the right to go to a white school if they want to?"

"Why would they want to? Why ask for trouble?" her father replied. He looked exasperated.

Gary considered her with surprise. "Thanks, Sylvie. I thought you were scared of integration."

"I am. Terrified. Crazy scared. But what you're saying might be right." She picked at the eggs on her plate.

"Horace Mann was just built last year," Mr. Patterson countered, drumming his fingers on the tablecloth. "It's pretty nice, isn't it?"

"Yeah, but it's not as nice as Central!" Gary retorted. "Our schools are *segregated*, Dad! They built Mann just to keep us out of Central High School and the rest of *their* high schools! Don't you get it?"

"Oh, I understand, son, more than you know. You have no idea what indignities I have had to endure in my life. I, too, was an angry young man like you. But I swallowed my anger." His father's face looked pained.

"That can't be healthy, Dad," Gary said.

"Segregation *is* the law," Mrs. Patterson said then. "You must admit, son, that it would be very hard to fight against something that the majority of folks think is the way things are supposed to be."

"Who passed that law? White folks!" Gary declared angrily. "Well, my fight is just beginning! Segregation in schools is unfair, and since 1954 it *has* been illegal!"

"There's a lot more to think about than new desks, Gary," his father said gently. "If they decide to integrate the schools here in Little Rock, it won't be easy. There will be strong opposition, even violence. I don't want you to get hurt."

"Folks like Mrs. Crandall and her anti-integration committee have lots of power," Mrs. Patterson added. "They sip sweet tea over there in her kitchen, while they make plans for keeping the races apart. The latest I heard, they were telling folks that white children might catch some kind of disease if they go to school with black children."

"They are the ones suffering from a disease," Mr. Patterson said as he buttered his pancakes. "But what pill will get rid of the hatred they've got inside?"

"I'm not afraid of white people," Gary said, pouting a little. "They go to the bathroom just like we do!"

"Gary!" Mrs. Patterson said sharply. "I will not have you talking nasty at the breakfast table, or anywhere else. Apologize!"

Picturing Mr. Crandall on the toilet nearly made Sylvia giggle, but she held it in.

Gary mumbled something that sounded like "sorry," then he said, quite clearly, "I heard one of the Crandalls' dogs got into some poison last night. The word on the street is it died."

Sylvia looked up from her plate of eggs. *He wouldn't. He couldn't. Did he?*

"How do you know that, son?" his mother asked carefully.

"I was at Anita's last night. Her father told me," Gary replied.

"Was it the dog that bit me?" Donna Jean asked, her voice almost hopeful.

"I don't know, DJ, but I hope it was," Gary told her. He asked to be excused from the table then. The lovely breakfast mood had been destroyed.

"What's gonna happen, Daddy?" Donna Jean asked.

"Nothing, child. Nothing. The price is too high." Her father stood and stretched, but he didn't look very relaxed.

"I don't get it, Sylvie," Donna Jean said, leaning over. "Isn't it *better* to go to school with kids who look like you and know what you're talking about when you say you got nappy hair or ashy legs?"

Sylvia laughed. "Look at it this way, DJ," she began, "the doors to schools like Central High are all locked up. Only the white kids get to have keys. If Gary decides that he wants to open one of those doors, he ought to have the right to do it. You see?"

"Yeah, I guess." She folded her napkin and pushed away from the table. "Is Rachel coming over on Saturday?" she asked, changing the subject.

Sylvia nodded. "Yeah. She and I are going to paint our fingernails and toenails. Bright red."

"That's dumb. You gotta wear shoes and socks. Who's gonna know you have pretty toes?" Donna Jean picked up a stack of plates. "Besides, Mama won't let you wear red finger-nail polish. She'll say you look like a floozy."

"Mama wouldn't know a floozy if she rang the doorbell, and you wouldn't, either," Sylvia said with a laugh. "I'll do my nails in pale pink. She'll never see my toes!"

Donna Jean paused and looked at her sister. "Hey, Sylvie, does Rachel have one of those keys you talked about?"

"Yep! A key, a magic door opener, and an engraved initiation to enter!" Sylvia admitted with a sigh. "Now go read a book, since you're so eager to go back to school." Donna Jean disappeared behind the swinging door. Sylvia picked up the cups and glasses and listened to her parents' worried tones.

"Gary's got the will and the spirit to fight this battle, Leola," Mr. Patterson said quietly.

"I know, Lester. He's got the fire, but not the gentle breeze to control it. I'm afraid he'll get consumed by the blaze." Sylvia watched her mother continue to sweep the already spotlessly clean floor.

Friday, January 4, 1957

For as long as I can remember, Gary has been pushing the edges. In the summer, when the whole town is like a bowl of hot broth, he wants to know why he can't swim in the pool with the white children. He wants to know why gas station restrooms have toilets marked "white" and "colored." When we were younger, Gary once used the white bathroom—on purpose—and got Daddy in lots of trouble. The police-man yelled at Daddy like he was a little boy, told him to make his children behave. Daddy kept saying, "Yes, sir," but I could see in his eyes he was really upset. Later I heard him tell Mama that he had to pray till the rage flew away.

Gary doesn't pray. He does stuff—usually before he thinks. I'm pretty sure he killed that dog.

Gary doesn't like it when Rachel comes to visit. He slams doors and leaves, which is fine with me. She is my only white friend, and surprisingly, she and I are really pretty close considering we live in two different worlds just a few blocks away from each other. We go to different schools, of course, and I go to church every Sunday, while she goes to synagogue every Saturday. We first met when we were four or five, and we see each other at least twice a month.

The Zucker family is one of just a few Jewish families in town. They own a local grocery store, which is right next door to Crandall's barbershop. On the other side of Zucker's store is Miss Lillie's flower shop. I can bet money that Mr. Crandall has never set foot in her store, even though he's only two doors down. I've never seen Miss Lillie Cobbs dressed in any color but green. She's tall and thin and looks like a flower when I squint. She does the floral arrangements for all the colored weddings and funerals, and she brings fresh flowers for the church every Sunday. She makes her son Calvin carry the heavy bouquets. It's fun to watch him because he likes to act so silly.

Mama shops at Zucker's grocery all the time because Mr. Zucker treats her with respect. He is the only white man I know who says, "Yes, ma'am," to Mama when he speaks to her. Mrs. Zucker, who is big and cheerful and sells her fresh-baked cakes and pastries at the store, always gives me a big hug and a free cookie. It's one of those hugs that envelops your whole head and you almost can't breathe while she's doing it, but it's not a bad thing because you know her heart is in the right place.

When we were kids Rachel and I would run up and down the polished wooden aisles of the store, playing hide-and-seek among the canned goods and boxes of baking soda, laughing like little kids do, rarely thinking about our differences. She once asked me, "Why are your arms and legs brown like that? And if you wash, will the brown come off?" I wasn't sure what to say. So I just said, "I'm brown and pretty, just the way God made me. Why would I want to wash it off?" I guess she didn't know what to say after that, so we never talked about it again. It didn't really matter between us.

She and I talk on the phone pretty regularly, and we still like to laugh about the same things, but as we get older, sometimes the conversation gets a little strained. I've never asked her what she thinks about integration.

I know the Jewish folk in town are mistreated sometimes, too. It's hard to understand why some white folks hate the Jews so much. Mr. Crandall, for example, refuses to cut Mr. Zucker's hair in his shop. I don't get it. It's not like Jewish folks look different from other white people, like we do.

I once saw Mr. Crandall spit in his hand just before he offered it to Mr. Zucker at his grocery store. I don't think Mr. Zucker saw him do it, because he offered his hand to Mr. Crandall with a smile.

SATURDAY, JANUARY 5, 1957

Sylvia and Donna Jean, after cleaning their room and putting fresh chenille bedspreads on their twin beds, sat down and turned on the transistor radio. Elvis Presley's "You Ain't Nothin' but a Hound Dog" was playing for what seemed to be the millionth time.

"Do you like Elvis?" Donna Jean asked Sylvia.

"I guess so. Everybody does. His songs sound a lot like colored music, don't you think?"

"I don't really know," Donna Jean replied. "I don't think I'll ever learn the names of all the singers and their songs like you do. How will I ever be popular in junior high if I can't tell the difference between Fats Domino and Perry Como?"

Sylvia laughed. "Well, Fats Domino is fat and loud and colored; while Perry Como is quiet and very white and sings love songs. Rachel thinks he's the most! Learning all that stuff just comes with practice. I pretend at school all the time that I know what I'm talking about. I think lots of the other girls do, too."

"So colored people don't sing pretty love songs?" Donna Jean looked confused.

"Sure they do. 'Why Do Fools Fall in Love' by Frankie Lymon is one of my favorites. Now he's somebody who is good-looking—and the same age as me!"

"I wonder how he got to be a rock-and-roll star," Donna Jean mused.

"I don't know, but I can tell you one thing—he doesn't have a father like Daddy!" Both girls laughed as Little Richard's "Tutti Frutti" began to play.

"Sylvia Faye! Turn that devil music down!" their father shouted up the stairs. "How is a man supposed to think with all that foolishness blasting through his house?" Sylvia noticed he didn't really sound angry, nor did he ask her to turn it off completely.

"Sorry, Daddy!" Sylvia called to him. Both girls giggled, but Sylvia immediately decreased the volume a bit.

Donna Jean winced a little as she walked over to the window and looked out at the chilly afternoon. "I wonder where Gary's going," she mused. "He looks like he's in a hurry."

"He wants to make sure he's long gone before Rachel gets here. How's your leg?" Sylvia asked with concern as she joined her sister.

Donna Jean looked serious for a moment. "It only hurts a little bit—I'll be fine." Then she looked up at Sylvia and asked, "If they integrate the schools, how will we talk about stuff that only we understand, like colored singers and dancers and stuff?"

"I have no idea, DJ, but I have a feeling that talking about singers and dancers would be one of the last things to worry about. Staying alive while going to classes would probably be up there on the top of the list."

Donna Jean touched her bandage. "That's scary. Would you want to be one of the first people to integrate a big old school like Central?" Donna Jean turned the radio back up a little as a Fats Domino song began to play. "Now this is one I know!" she said happily. "I found my thrill," she sang softly with the record, "on Blueberry Hill . . ."

"Well, going to Central High would certainly be no thrill. It would be a real test of courage, and I don't think I have any." Sylvia hummed along with the song.

"What if Gary gets picked to go to Central?" DJ asked, frowning.

"Not a pretty picture," Sylvia replied as she flopped down on her pillow. "Would he refuse to fight if they pushed him? Put up with nasty comments from smart-mouthed white kids?"

"Not likely," DJ said. "He'd end up in jail for sure."

Just then their mother came into the room with freshly laundered towels. "After you put these away, come down and help me freshen the living room," she said. "Rachel will be here soon, and I want this house spotless."

Sylvia didn't hurry—she knew the house was ridiculously clean. "Mama, tell us again about when you were in school," Sylvia asked as she folded the towels. It was fun to imagine her mother as a kid.

Her mother looked out the window and a smile crossed her face. "When I was the age of you girls, everybody I knew went to the schools built just for colored kids, just like you do now. We used books the white schools had thrown out, desks they no longer wanted, and materials that were outdated and torn, but we didn't care. We didn't *want* to go to school with the white kids. We had strong, powerful Negro teachers like Miss Washington who taught us pride in ourselves, confidence in our abilities, and all the academic skills we needed. When I went to college, I finished first in my class at an integrated university. I had been well prepared."

"Things are changing, aren't they, Mama?" Donna Jean asked quietly.

"Yes, baby girl. Change is heading for us like a runaway truck."

Just then the doorbell rang. "That's Rachel! I'll get it!" Sylvia said, jumping up from her bed. "Can you keep DJ in the kitchen while Rachel is here, Mama? We have girl stuff to talk about."

"I'm a girl, too!" Donna Jean said defiantly, her arms folded across her chest.

"Come help me make the apple pie, Donna Jean. You've got lots of time to be a teenager," her mother said smoothly.

Sylvia bounded down the stairs to open the door, waved to Rachel's mother, who was just driving off, and gave her friend a hug. Rachel wore a turquoise-colored poodle skirt decorated with silver music notes, black vinyl records, and two white teenagers dancing. "I *love* your skirt!" Sylvia said. "I've got to get one of those!"

Rachel stamped the slushy snow off her saddle oxfords and took off her jacket. She grinned and twirled around to show the full effect of the huge circular skirt. "I brought the nail polish," she said.

"Good." The two girls walked into the living room and plopped down on the plastic-covered sofa. "Hey, what is it with mothers that they buy this nice furniture then cover it all up?" Sylvia asked as she traced the pattern of the well-covered fabric. "My mother had these custom-made so they'd fit the couch exactly!"

Rachel laughed. "I once asked my mother why she covered all our furniture with plastic. She told me it was to keep it nice and clean and that way if we had company, it would look like new."

"My mom says the same thing. But I have never, ever seen her take it off, not even when ladies from church come over. They all have this stuff on their living room furniture, too. When I grow up, I'm going to let my children sit on the sofa with no plastic to stick to their legs," Sylvia said with confidence.

"I like the way your mom lines up your magazines," Rachel said. "My mom just throws them in a basket by her favorite chair." Mrs. Patterson had arranged the stacks into three neat diagonal piles on the small coffee table, so the edges made a little pattern—one for *Look* magazine, one for *Life*, and one for *Ebony.*

Sylvia picked up a copy of *Ebony.* "I bet you don't have this one at your house!" she said with a slight smile.

"You're right there," Rachel said. "My father gets newspapers printed in German, but my mother subscribes to *Life* and *Reader's Digest.*"

"I like *Ebony* because everybody in the whole magazine is colored—even in the ads."

Rachel looked a little uncomfortable and picked up a copy of *Life.* "Regardless of what color the people are, don't you think the ads are stupid? Look at this one—a clothes dryer with a built-in sunlamp that will get your clothes thirty-four percent fluffier. How do they measure stuff like that?"

Sylvia chuckled. "All I know is the pile of towels in that pictures is a lot taller than any pile I've seen of our towels hanging in our backyard to dry!"

Rachel nodded and flipped through the magazine. "Look at this one!" She read it in the singsong voice of a television announcer. "Housework fatigue? If you feel headachy and irritable after a busy day of housework, take Bayer aspirin to relieve your pain. You'll feel better fast—ready for a pleasant evening with your husband." Both girls rolled with laughter.

"What's *that* supposed to mean?" Sylvia asked, giggling.

"When you marry Reggie, you'll find out!" Rachel replied in a teasing tone.

"Mama and Daddy are so strict that I'll probably be old

and dried up by the time they let me actually go out on a date, let alone get married!" Sylvia complained. "But Reggie Birmingham sure is cute!"

"My folks are stupid strict like that, too," Rachel said. "And in no hurry to get me hitched. I've been told since I was a little girl that when I'm twenty-one I can *start* looking for a nice Jewish boy to marry."

"Suppose you fell in love with a Catholic kid?"

"They'd have a heart attack."

"What about a colored kid?" Sylvia asked, teasing.

"They'd probably roll over and die," Rachel answered with a giggle.

"Mine are like that, too. Old folks have issues," Sylvia commented.

Mrs. Patterson came in then with a plate of brownies and two glasses of milk. "I wonder what my life will be like when and if I get married," Rachel mused when Mrs. Patterson left the room. "It seems like my mother is never really happy."

"I know what you mean. I wonder if my mother dreamed of a rich man and pretty children and a fancy house like I do. Instead she got Daddy, who's a little overweight; and us, just ordinary kids; and our small gray house, which is nothing like the houses I see in *Life* or *Ebony* magazine. I wonder if she ever gets tired of it all."

"My mother worries a lot—mostly about things out of her control. She doesn't sleep well," Rachel said.

Sylvia nodded in agreement. "Late on Saturday night, I can hear my mother still fixing and cleaning. She never rests. I don't know when she does her own hair, or irons her clothes, or even when she goes to bed. All I know is she's always up before we are, and there's a big breakfast ready on the table—French toast with Alaga syrup, fried eggs, grits, and cold glasses of milk. Do wives ever have any fun?"

Rachel had no answer. They ate their brownies in silence.

Saturday, January 5, 1957
Rachel and I had a good time today. Mama still hasn't seen my red toenails. Some stuff you just hide. Rachel's dad wears long-sleeved shirts and a tie every day, even in summer, and sometimes it's hard for me to understand him when he speaks to me because he talks in a thick German accent. But every once in a while when the weather turns unbearably hot, he rolls up his shirtsleeves. I have seen the purple numbers tattooed on his forearm.

Sometimes Mama buys fresh beef from Mr. Zucker, and it's always marked with a large purple stamp of quality. I used to think the mark on Mr. Zucker's arm was something that had happened accidentally while he was preparing the meat. But the mark never faded and never came off. I think I was about eight when I asked him what that mark meant. Mr. Zucker said one word—Auschwitz. At the time I didn't know what that meant, but the look of despair in his eyes scared me. He never said anything else about it, and I never dared to ask.

I've heard my parents whisper about a Jewish man named Leo Frank who got lynched in Georgia a few years ago. Almost every colored family can tell a story about someone they knew who was taken out at midnight by an angry mob and hung by a rope until they died. My father rarely talks about what happened to my grandfather, but I know he was hung from an apple tree, and my dad witnessed it all. I see the leftover hurt that wraps around Daddy like a shawl.

Even teenagers can get lynched. Just two years ago a boy about my age named Emmett Till was murdered in Mississippi. He was from Chicago, and was visiting some relatives. According to the story he bought some candy in a little store and spoke to the owner's wife with disrespect. His Mississippi friends couldn't believe this Northern boy who had so much nerve. Two days later he was dragged out of his house in the middle of the night by two men. Emmett's body was found three days later in a river with a huge piece of machinery tied around his neck. He had been beaten, shot, drowned, and tortured—one of his eyes had been gouged out.

It was in all the papers and everybody in town had an opinion. I heard some white folks say it was his fault because he should have known better, but other white folks said it was an outrage—that Mississippi folks just go too far. All the colored folks I knew were angry and scared. If a teenager from Chicago could get lynched, what chance did we have here in Arkansas? Anyway, they arrested the men who had taken him, but they were found not guilty at the trial. White folks expected that outcome. Colored folks knew not to expect better.

The thing I'll never forget about that story is that *Jet* magazine showed the picture of Emmett Till's dead body. His mother had insisted on having an open-casket funeral—she said she wanted the world to see what they had done to her boy. There he lay in his coffin, wearing a nice suit and tie. But that's all that was pleasant about that picture. His head was swollen and grotesque from being in the water so long. One eye was missing, one side of his head was crushed, and a hole, I guess from a bullet, distorted his nose. He didn't look like a teenager, like the good-looking boy with the cheerful smile they showed on the other page—he looked liked a monster. Mama told me it was monsters that did that to him, but it didn't help much. I remember not being able to sleep well for weeks after that. It still bothers me—now, more than ever.

It was a little cold in the classroom on their first day back from the holidays. The heat had been turned off for two weeks, and it sometimes took it a couple of days to kick back in. Mr. Nathaniel, the janitor, told the students to be patient and to keep their coats on until it warmed up. The boiler was located right beneath the classroom, so Sylvia and the rest of her class could hear him tinkering around with it.

Just before nine, the students heard a clunky noise like a large piece of metal falling on a cement floor, followed by a very loud, very clear string of curse words from Mr. Nathaniel. He hollered up to them, "Hey, sorry about that," but by then the whole class was laughing.

She glanced over at Reggie, who wore a brown bomber jacket, brown corduroy pants, and a pair of well-worn, dark blue Keds tennis shoes. One white sock peeked through the hole in the right shoe, and the rubber was peeling off the left shoe. Reggie was whispering something to Candace Castle, who seemed to be one of those girls who would, without hesitation, be found kissing a boy behind the high school. *There's a reason the boys call her Candy*, Sylvia thought with a frown. She looked down at her book and pretended to read.

Miss Ethel Washington, their English and Social Studies teacher, who was a stern, unsmiling woman with large hips and a tiny waist, got the class quiet and serious with a glance. She was tall and plump, and from what Sylvia could tell, probably close to sixty years old. She had taught many of their parents and a few of their grandparents as well.

Her black hair, streaked with lots of gray, was pulled back tightly into a bun on her neck. She wore large brown glasses, which fell to the tip of her nose when she asked a question in class, and sturdy brown shoes. Her dresses, made of stiff fabric in various shades of black or gray or brown, never seemed to wrinkle. Sylvia had also never seen Miss Washington wear a brightly colored or a flowered dress. She figured a painted rose or a daisy just might wilt, like one of Miss Lillie's leftover buds, if it had to lie that close to the body of Miss Ethel Washington!

Calvin Cobbs, Miss Lillie's son, didn't take anything too seriously, and joked around as much as he dared in Miss Washington's class. He whispered to Sylvia, "Miss Ethel woulda been a good army sergeant!" He chuckled at his own joke. Still laughing, he added, "Forget that—she would have made a good army truck!"

Sylvia put her hand over her mouth so Calvin couldn't see her smile. "You better hope she doesn't hear you!" she told Calvin softly.

"In old people, hearing is the first to go," Calvin replied, not even whispering anymore. "There is no way the old bird knows what I'm saying." He grinned at Sylvia, a look of careless confidence on his face.

"Please specify the bird to which you are referring, Mr. Cobbs," Miss Washington said suddenly as she loomed over his desk.

Calvin shrank in his seat, his tan-colored, freckled face turning an odd shade of maroon. Sylvia shook her head and smiled to herself. Calvin got in trouble for his good-natured joking around almost every day, but he always bounced back.

"Uh, bird? I was just asking Sylvia if she had *heard* anything about the integration of the schools," he explained weakly. Then, turning the conversation to a subject he knew the teacher would like, he asked her, "So, Miss Washington, what do you think of segregated schools?"

The teacher gave him her over-the-nose-and-through-the-glasses piercing stare, then replied, "Why don't you ask the Supreme Court of this country what they think, Mr. Cobbs?" *He's in for it now!* Sylvia watched with amusement.

Calvin squirmed in his seat. "Uh, I can go to the library and find out," he answered weakly.

"Not necessary. What decision was rendered on May 17, 1954, Mr. Cobbs?" Miss Washington demanded with a glare that dared him to answer incorrectly.

"Brown v. the Board of Education of Topeka, Kansas," Calvin replied, almost trembling.

"And what did it say?" Miss Washington continued.

"Uh, it said that separate but equal schools are illegal." The teacher seemed to relax a little then, but Calvin had never figured out how to quit when he was ahead. So he asked then, "So how come it's been three years and we still have segregated schools in Little Rock?"

Miss Washington glanced out of the window and said nothing for a few moments. The class was absolutely quiet, waiting for her response. Finally she said to Calvin, "If you would stop your foolishness in class, Mr. Cobbs, and apply yourself to your studies, you could become a lawyer like Mr. Thurgood Marshall and help to implement that law."

"All I wanna do is grow flowers like my mom and make

folks laugh like my dad. I don't want to change the world," Calvin muttered. "I should've kept my mouth shut."

Miss Washington continued. "Actually, I'm glad you brought it up, Mr. Cobbs. As you all know, back in 1954, the school board here in Little Rock said it would comply with the Supreme Court when they figured out how and when integration would take place here in our city. And I know that you're aware that last year, when twenty-six Negro students tried to register in the white schools, they were turned down."

"My cousin was in that group!" Calvin offered. "She ain't scared of nothing!"

"That should be *isn't* and *anything*," Miss Washington corrected automatically. "There's going to be plenty to be scared of, Mr. Cobbs, if it really happens this time." She paused and sighed. "Although I think they hoped it would never happen, the school board has finally decided that integration will begin gradually this coming September, starting with the high school students, and adding the lower grades over the next few years."

"Are they gonna shut down our schools and make us all go to school with the white kids?" Reggie asked. He sounded concerned. "I *like* the fact that Dunbar and Mann are just for the colored kids! They don't want us and we don't need them."

"No, Mr. Birmingham. This process may take years. Next week we will start the selection process for those of you who might choose to be among the first, the proud, maybe even the famous. But it will not be easy. The white establishment does not want you there. It will be difficult, maybe even painful, and probably dangerous. I want you to go home tonight and talk to your parents. After much discussion and prayer, if you and your family wants to be considered for this, I want you to let me know. We are slowly compiling a list of possible students to present to the school board. Only the best and the brightest will be chosen. Will you be among them?"

"I know I don't want to be on that list," Sylvia heard Reggie say.

The bell rang then, and Sylvia exhaled as if she had been underwater. Integration! Here in Little Rock. Finally. And she and her friends could be the ones chosen to do it. What a terrible, horrible, wonderful decision this would be.

Monday, January 7, 1957—afternoon
Some of the students in my class don't like Miss Washington because they think she's mean, and others are just plain scared of her. She hardly ever smiles, and she looms over students like a grizzly bear over its prey, almost growling sometimes when we sound stupid. I wouldn't want to be trapped in a cave with her, but I'm not afraid of her, and I know she's tough on us so we can make it in a rough world.

She tells us all the time that we have to be better prepared than the white children so that we can compete for jobs and opportunities. She told us she refuses to send incompetent, unprepared Negroes into a world that expects us to mess up in the first place. So she drills us constantly—grammar and vocabulary, states and capitals, continents and constellations, even the United States Constitution.

Every single one of us—even Calvin Cobbs—can recite the Gettysburg Address and long passages of Shakespeare. We can spell and define every single one of the words on Miss Washington's famous one-thousand-word list, and can probably conjugate irregular verbs in our sleep. When she's teaching, she beats on the blackboard with her yard-stick, and roars at us to learn and remember and recite. So we do.

And it's still just January. I don't tell my friends, but I like her challenges and her demands. Although I don't know how I'll be able to afford it, I want to go to college. Miss Washington has never said she thought I was smart or anything, but I notice that she expects for me to have the right answers, even when other students get stuck.

Miss Ethel Washington also talks to us about real things—like how to survive in a segregated world. I think she may have gone through some terrible experiences in her life—something to make her so stern and formal and unsmiling. I wonder what she really thinks of all this talk about integration.

Miss Washington has also taught me to love poetry. I know dozens of poems by Paul Laurence Dunbar and Langston Hughes, as well as Walt Whitman and Robert Frost. She once posted one of my poems in the main hall during a parent open house event. Even though I didn't think the poem was that great, I was really proud. Mama cried, because the poem was about her.

MY MOTHER'S GARDEN

She tends us like hyacinths—
    Delicate sprouts, fragile buds,
      Determined we will bloom.
Fiercely she rips the weeds
    from around us—
No ragged, uncultured
    piece of greengrowth

would ever dare to approach us.
We are carefully mulched in the winter
with composted piles of hard-swept dust—
to protect us from
winter storms or sudden rains or
frosty unseen chills in the night.
In the spring
we bloom with smiles and sunshine,
we flower into tall, healthy blossoms,
and we dance in the gentle soft rains of her love.

Sylvia Faye Patterson

MONDAY, JANUARY 7, 1957—EVENING

How was your first day back to school, DJ?" Sylvia asked as she sat on her bed to start her homework.

"Pretty good! All the kids thought my bandage was really neat, and it didn't hurt me at all," Donna Jean replied.

"So you were the center of attention?"

"Right where I like to be!" her sister replied, a look of victory on her face.

"It helps that Mama is your teacher," Sylvia said. "I used to like it when I was in her class. I always felt safe."

"Is Daddy home yet?" Donna Jean asked.

"No, he had to work at the brickyard for a couple of hours," Sylvia told her. She knew he often came home from his second job at Dimming's Brickyard feeling tired, grumpy.

"He never talks about that job," DJ said. "Does he make bricks there, or what?"

"He sweeps up, that's all," Sylvia explained. "Daddy never gets to make or lay any bricks. You have to be in the union for that and Negroes can't join."

"That's not fair!" DJ exclaimed.

"So what else is new?" Sylvia replied with a sigh.

"Are we poor, Sylvie?"

"What made you ask that, DJ?"

"Well, we've got a really old, ugly car!" Donna Jean laughed. "And we're always looking for dimes in the sofa cushions so we can buy gas."

Sylvia hated their big black 1949 Chevrolet. It had a rounded front that looked like a nose, and a humped back. "That's because Daddy is so cheap!" Sylvia replied with a laugh. "But you're right, DJ. The new cars are so much sleeker. Those long fins make them look like they can fly down the road. Our car just plods along like an old donkey."

"It looks like a bear," Donna Jean said, walking around the room hunched over and growling.

"Daddy complains every time he has to put gas in it that he's going to go broke if he has to keep paying twenty-four cents a gallon."

"Is that a lot?"

"I think it's like a full day's wage. I read in the newspaper that the minimum wage is supposed to be a dollar an hour, but that must be only for white folks."

"Do you know how much money Mama and Daddy make?" Donna Jean asked.

"I'm not sure, but I know that teachers at the colored school make about half as much as teachers in the white schools. And I know that women teachers make less than men."

"For real? Is that fair?"

"Not much seems to be fair these days. At least Daddy gets a portion of the church donations. But when people are going through hard times, Daddy's pay goes through hard times, too."

Donna Jean was about to answer, but Mrs. Patterson called them down to dinner. Their father had come home early, and seemed to be in a good mood. He kissed her mother on the cheek, gave Sylvia and Donna Jean big hugs, and grabbed a piece of corn bread off the plate. He gobbled half of it before his wife had a chance to pretend like she was going to fuss at him. He grinned at his family and stuffed the rest of it into his mouth while everybody laughed.

"Now you see where Gary gets his eating habits," their mother teased, laughing with them.

"Where is that boy, anyway?" Mr. Patterson asked. The mood suddenly darkened, almost as if a shadow had slid across the kitchen linoleum.

Her mother said nothing, but kept glancing out the kitchen curtains, hoping that Gary would turn the corner with his long legs and swaggering walk.

"He'll be here soon, Lester," she said as she placed the rest of the food on the table. "Maybe he had some extra work to do at school."

Her parents were aware that was really unlikely, Sylvia knew. She scooped up a big pile of mashed potatoes and plopped a large pat of butter right in the middle of it. She loved it when the butter melted into the potatoes—she swirled it around and watched the colors and flavors collide. Besides, she figured that playing with her food was preferable to bringing up the subject of the integration of Central High School right now.

Mr. Patterson prayed a long time before the meal, asking the Lord to keep his family safe in these difficult times. Nobody said much as they ate, but each person at the table kept glancing at the door, waiting for the next shadow to fall.

It came with a thud and a curse. Mrs. Patterson stifled a scream when they heard an object hit their front porch. Sylvia thought it sounded soft, but heavy, like a large bag of fruit. The curse came as they ran to the door—three white boys ran down their driveway, cackling and shouting as they jumped into a black '56 Ford and sped away.

When Sylvia's father opened the front door, there lay Gary, curled like a bruised animal. Both his eyes were swollen and puffy, his nose was bleeding, and Sylvia saw cuts and bruises all over his head and arms. He held his arms tightly around his chest. Mrs. Patterson, once again calm in the face of calamity, didn't lose her composure.

"Sylvia, take Donna Jean upstairs, then get me some hot water and bandages. Hurry." Donna Jean, her eyes wide with fear, didn't object.

Mr. Patterson, his face a mask of pain and anger, lifted Gary up as if he were a baby and brought him inside.

"Should I call the doctor?" Sylvia asked as she hurried back down the stairs.

"Not yet," her mother said. "Let me see how bad it is."

"What about the police?" Sylvia asked.

"Absolutely not," her father replied strongly.

"But, Daddy, you can't let them get away with this! We have a colored policeman now. Can't we call him?" Sylvia's eyes flashed in anger. She remembered a unit her class had covered in second grade called, "The Policeman Is Our Friend," where a smiling and very white police officer directed traffic and helped little old white ladies across the street.

"He can't even issue tickets, and for sure he's not allowed to arrest a white person. Forget it!" her father said harshly.

While her mother washed Gary's wounds with warm water, Sylvia shook her head in disbelief. They had just endured this scene with Donna Jean a few days ago. It was like seeing a bad movie repeated in their living room. Sylvia shuddered, wondering if next it would be *her* bloody body that her mother would be soothing on the sofa, trying in vain to bandage up the hatred that caused it.

Gary looked up and said through puffy lips, "I'm sorry, Mama."

"What happened, son?" his father asked. Sylvia hovered nearby, hoping she wouldn't be sent out of the room like Donna Jean.

"I made a couple of stops on my way home. I needed to talk to people who really know what's going on."

"Why didn't you just come straight home?" his mother asked.

"I should be safe in my own town, Mama," Gary said gently. "I shouldn't have to be scared to go anyplace I want to."

"Such a hardheaded child you are," his mother said, weeping. "You've always been my headstrong, bold baby. But it's going to get you killed, Gary."

"Don't cry, Mama. I'll be fine. I promise I'll be more careful." Gary reached up to touch his mother's face.

"So where did you go?" his father asked. He was pacing the floor again.

"I stopped by the NAACP office to see if there was any news about the school integration stuff."

"No wonder they targeted you!" his father roared. "Why do you hang around those people?"

"Because when they choose students to go, I intend to be one of them!" Gary replied with as much vigor as his injuries would allow.

"Well, this certainly isn't going to help your chances!" Mr. Patterson retorted angrily. "Even if we decided to let you try!"

"It wasn't my fault!" Gary protested. "I was almost home—walking down the street, minding my own business, when those three boys started calling me 'Nigger' and 'Coon.' One of them was Johnny Crandall. The other two were Sonny and Bubba Smith. They were in a car, but they followed me real slow, yelling and cursing the whole time."

Everybody knew not to tangle with the Smith brothers. They called themselves the "Wild Cherry Cough Drops," and had been known to vandalize cars and steal from the Zuckers' market. They took great pleasure in driving their '56 Ford up and down the streets of the Negro neighborhood all night long. The car had no muffler, so it sounded like a mechanical animal in distress, and a very loud, specially installed horn blared the song "Dixie" so loudly it could be heard blocks away.

"Couldn't you just have ignored them, son?" his mother asked tearfully as she bandaged the cuts on his head. "Doesn't the Good Book tell us to turn the other cheek?"

"I tried, Mama, but then they started throwing beer cans at me, so I picked up one of the cans and threw it back. It hit Bubba Smith in his eye." It looked to Sylvia like Gary was trying to smile, but his lip was pretty swollen by this time. "They stopped the car, jumped out, and even though I got in a couple of good punches, I couldn't stop all three of them."

"How did they know where you live?" his father asked.

"They know, Dad. They know. They tossed me back on my own porch to send a message. They know I'll never stop fighting for what's right!"

"Unless they kill you," Mr. Patterson said angrily.

Sylvia wasn't sure if her father was angry at Gary, or at the boys who attacked him, but at no time that evening did she see him get on his knees and pray. And, for once, her mother had no proverbs to quote.

Monday, January 7, 1957—Late Evening

I really worry about my big brother. His wounds will heal, but not the fury that keeps growing inside his heart. Gary is angry all the time these days. When he used to sing in the choir at church, his face would almost glow with happiness. But lately, that's not been very often.

I'm supposed to be asleep now. Donna Jean is snuggled in her bed snoring, and the rest of the house is quiet now. After Daddy helped Gary upstairs, he and my mother talked for a long time. I couldn't hear what they were saying, but their voices were upset. Mama, I'm sure, wants to protect Gary and move someplace safe like Alaska or Arabia—anyplace that's not Arkansas. Her motherly instincts are to put a big blanket around him and make sure nothing hurts him. Only there's no covering large enough to protect him from people like the Smith brothers or the Crandalls. Mama once told Gary to put his anger in a pot and let it simmer. He told her that one day he'd come to a boil. Mama looked a little scared and changed the subject.

I bet Daddy would love to punch one of those kids right in the nose. Pow! Then watch him bleed. I think he'd feel better if he could act on what's inside him. But I don't think he'd ever forgive himself if he did. He's been a preacher too long. Besides, they'd throw him in jail, he'd lose both his jobs, and Mama would die of shame.

But if nobody cries out for change, nothing will happen. I don't want to grow up and have to drive ten miles past the pretty school to take my kids to the ratty old building where the colored kids have to go. I don't want my daughter to look at me with pity while some white shopkeeper insults me.

Mama makes all her own clothes, and most of our clothes, too. She does this because it costs a lot less, but also because it's often embarrassing to go to a store to buy things. I don't think it's fair that Negroes have to keep what they buy, while white folks get to try it on at the store, or at their house, then return it a couple of weeks later if they change their mind. Mama says there was a time when we couldn't shop in the stores at all. I guess that's progress, but it doesn't seem like it to me.

That's it for tonight. I'm going to be a mess in school tomorrow if I don't get some sleep.

So, have you called Reggie yet?" Lou Ann asked as she stirred the gravy into her potatoes.

Sylvia and Lou Ann Johnson, a skinny girl with a powerful laugh and a large gap between her front teeth, sat together most days at lunch. Lou Ann made low-to-average grades, always had boys following her around, and never seemed to have a bad day. She had been going steady with Otis Herman since the beginning of eighth grade. She wasn't going to be asked to consider Central High, and Sylvia knew she wouldn't have given it a second thought if she had.

Lou Ann's father, Zeke, owned the barbershop where most of the Negro men in town got their hair cut. She always had money in her purse, and never brought her lunch. She'd buy the Salisbury steak with gravy that the cafeteria offered, plus an ice-cream sandwich, which the students made themselves out of two freshly baked sugar cookies with a square of vanilla ice cream stuck between them.

Lou Ann was always cheerful and carefree. Everything Otis said or did made her laugh, and she shared her laughter with her whole class. Sylvia knew Lou Ann was the right one to talk to.

"Oh, I couldn't call him first!" Sylvia said, sounding slightly shocked. "I'm waiting for him to call me. My mother says only bad girls call boys."

Lou Ann laughed heartily. "Do you always do what your mother says?"

Sylvia didn't want to admit that she usually did, so she

changed the subject. "I think Reggie is going to play football at Horace Mann next year. My brother told me."

"There's nothing more fun than a high school football game," Lou Ann said wistfully, sipping her milk. "The band, the music, the cheers and the cheerleaders, the roar of the crowd, the boys in their uniforms with those pants tight on their rear ends—simply too cool." She laughed again.

Sylvia wished she could be more like Lou Ann. She always said exactly what was on her mind, and never seemed to be bothered by the rules and regulations. "Uh, I never noticed," Sylvia said as she made her ice-cream sandwich. It was her custom to let the ice cream melt a little as she ate her lunch so that it would be soft enough to lick into a perfectly round, perfectly delicious treat.

"Well, if you didn't, you sure will when Reggie is playing!" Lou Ann replied with a laugh. She licked the mashed potatoes off her spoon. "If you don't use him, you'll lose him!"

"How can I lose something I don't even have?" Sylvia said helplessly. "Besides, I think he likes Candy Castle."

Lou Ann laughed so hard that little streams of milk came out of her nose. "Don't you know that *all* the boys like Candy? She's hot chocolate, Sylvia. Melted, sweet, soft, and delicious. That's why you have to let him know you like him. Boys go for quality, too—sometimes." Reggie walked across the cafeteria, carrying a tray and heading for a table where Calvin Cobbs and a couple of other boys sat. "Hey, Reggie!" Lou Ann called as loud as she could. "Come sit with us."

Sylvia felt herself shrivel as he grinned, changed direction, and headed their way. He wore a blue argyle sweater, blue chino slacks, and those raggedy blue Keds. The rubber of the left shoe flapped a little as he walked. "How could you do that?" she whispered to Lou Ann.

"Aw, quit acting like your little sister. Talk to the boy like you got some sense!" Lou Ann admonished.

"How do you get so many boys to notice you?" Sylvia asked Lou Ann shyly as she glanced with wonderment at Reggie's approach.

"I relax, Sylvia, like you need to do. Boys don't like tense girls. They dig someone who can make them feel good. You're too uptight."

Sylvia had no idea how to relax like Lou Ann suggested. She wondered if Reggie thought she was boring. There was just so much she couldn't figure out.

"How's it goin'?" Reggie asked, chewing that Juicy Fruit gum as he grinned. He sat down then, his long legs bumping Sylvia's under the table as he got situated. She gasped slightly and her heart thudded, but he didn't seem to be nervous at all.

"I'm fine, Reggie," Sylvia replied as smoothly as she could. "How's your brother doing on the Mann basketball team this year?"

"Greg thinks he's a superstar," Reggie said between mouthfuls of meat loaf. "Says he wants to play for the Harlem Globetrotters one day." Then, looking more serious, he said, "Speaking of brothers, I heard about Gary. How is he doing? Tell him if he ever needs help dealing with the white boys, I got his back!"

Why are boys so ready to fight all the time? Sylvia thought as she stirred her corn pudding. "He'll be okay—on the outside, at least." Sylvia frowned. "I think Gary is simply gonna crash and burn one day. Might get messy."

Reggie smiled. "He'll heal up. Then he'll be ready to fight again—stronger and tougher. But speaking of basketball," he said smoothly, "there's a game at Mann next week. Would you like to go with me?"

Sylvia almost choked on her cookies. She couldn't believe he was asking her on a date! She sat there for a moment, staring stupidly and saying nothing. Then she felt Lou Ann kick her leg.

"Uh, I'd have to ask my mother, but as long as she thinks there will be at least a million other people there, she might let me go."

"Cool!" he said. "Tell you what—to avoid the parent trap, why don't I just meet you there? Your folks can drop you off and pick you up, and neither one of us has to go through all those questions that parents think they have to ask."

"You sound like you've done this before!" Sylvia said, aware she was laughing too loudly.

Reggie, faking the deep bass voice of her father, said, "Now, tell me, son, what are your intentions concerning my darling daughter? And will you ever buy new shoes?"

Sylvia, Lou Ann, and Reggie, laughing hysterically, initially did not see Miss Washington approach. Sylvia looked up in surprise. Miss Washington, unsmiling and determined-looking, strode toward their table. Her sturdy shoes echoed on the linoleum floor. "I need to speak with you, Miss Patterson," she said brusquely. "Come with me."

Not now! Not in the middle of the most important conversa-

tion of my life! But all she could say was a polite and sorrowful, "Yes, ma'am."

Sylvia turned to Lou Ann with a shrug, gave Reggie an apologetic smile, and helplessly followed the ample hips of Miss Washington out of the cafeteria. Her heart thudded as she tried to imagine what she possibly could have done wrong. Usually it was Calvin Cobbs who was called to task for acting silly or forgetting his homework.

Maybe Sylvia had forgotten an important assignment in the confusion from last night. Gary's injuries, which, of course, everybody in the colored community had heard about by now, turned out to be mostly cuts and bruises, but he would be out of school for a few days. Maybe Miss Washington wanted to ask her about Gary. She'd had him in class a couple of years ago.

The voices of her friends echoed in the halls as they entered Miss Washington's empty and silent classroom.

"You're an excellent student, Miss Patterson," Miss Washington said, looking directly at her.

"Thank you, ma'am," she replied, a little surprised at the compliment. She felt like an ant under a magnifying glass.

"Have you discussed with your parents the opportunity I offered the class yesterday?"

"I didn't really get the chance, ma'am," Sylvia replied. "My brother, Gary, got into a little trouble last night, and Mama and Daddy were not in a mood to talk about Central High School."

"Yes, I heard about that. Gary always has been volatile and impetuous, and I must admit that his behavior might work against you. But you, my dear, are steady, dependable, and capable of handling the social and emotional difficulties that would confront you. We want your name to be placed on the list."

Sylvia was overwhelmed. "Me?" she croaked. "I don't think I'm brave enough for all that stuff."

"Yes, you are. In addition, you have intelligence, which the boys who attacked your brother do not have. Bravery and brains will take you a very long way."

"But it's Gary who wants to be on the list, not me. Choose him instead of me, please." Sylvia knew that Gary would kill for this chance, and they were offering it to her on a platter. He'd be furious when he found out—and hurt as well.

Miss Washington softened and smiled a little. "You are just the type of young woman who is needed for this task, Sylvia Faye." That was the first time she ever heard Miss Washington call a student by a first name.

Sylvia had to sit down at one of the empty desks. "My parents will never let me."

"I'll talk to them," Miss Washington interrupted. "I know they will have strong reservations because of the incident with Gary. But we'll see what happens. Go and finish your lunch now. And don't mention this conversation to anyone yet."

"Thank you, ma'am," Sylvia whispered as she hurried out of the room. She stood there in the hallway, trembling with apprehension. When she got back to the empty lunchroom, which smelled faintly of old meat loaf, both Reggie and Lou Ann had gone to their next class. Sylvia had lost her appetite anyway.

Sylvia knocked on Gary's door and peeked in his room. On his dartboard he had taped of picture of Orval Faubus, governor of Arkansas, a man who had made it very clear he did not like Negroes. Several darts had perforated the newspaper cutout.

"Does that make you feel better?" Sylvia asked, pointing at the dartboard as she walked in.

"Not really. But it gives me something to do for now," Gary told her. He was stuck at home until he was fully healed. It wouldn't be much longer. Most of the swelling had diminished considerably, and he only had a couple of Band-Aids still covering the deeper cuts on his arms. "So how was school today?"

Sylvia took a deep breath. "Same as usual. Except Reggie sat with me at lunch. He asked about you—said he'd back you up next time. That makes me real nervous, Gary."

"He understands the real deal," Gary said, nodding with approval. He gazed out of the darkened window.

"Reggie also asked me to go to a basketball game, and—"

"Ha! I told you he was sweet on you! Watch yourself. I know how bad boys can be when they like a girl," Gary warned.

"Uh, thanks, but Reggie's not like that. Besides, I don't think I have to worry as long as we're just sharing hot dogs at a game. There was one more thing, though." She hesitated. *How am I gonna tell him?*

"What? Miss Washington decided you should be on the debate team? You can't say no to that woman, you know."

"I know. But it wasn't the debate team." Sylvia paused, knew she was about to hurt him deeply, then she said slowly, "She wants me to be on the list of kids who might integrate Central High School." Sylvia felt miserable.

"That's great news!" Gary said as he got up to give Sylvia a hug. "We can go together, and I'll be there to protect you!"

It was even harder than she thought it would be. "Uh, I don't think they included your name, Gary. They're afraid you might be too outspoken or violent."

"Violent? Me?" Gary was predictably enraged. "Only if somebody starts it first. I don't let anybody push me around!"

"I think they know that," Sylvia said quietly. "I'm sorry, Gary. I didn't want this."

"It's not fair," Gary growled. "I *really* did."

She left his room, knowing he was the brave one, the bold one.

It was all she could think about as she helped her mother prepare the evening meal, and, although she opened her mouth to bring up the subject a couple of times, she simply didn't have the nerve to do it at dinner. Donna Jean chattered about the latest Archie comic book, unaware of the tension. Gary ate in silence.

After dinner Miss Washington didn't call—she showed up at their house. Sylvia was sitting on the sofa with Donna Jean, watching *The Dinah Shore Show* on TV. Gary was sitting in his father's favorite chair, still being spoiled by their mother. He refused to make eye contact with Sylvia.

The doorbell rang, and, since everyone in the family had been a bit jumpy lately, they turned off the television and waited for Mr. Patterson to answer it. Miss Ethel Washington filled the room with her authority. Sylvia jumped off the sofa, offered her seat to the teacher, and moved to a hassock where she waited for the firestorm that was sure to come.

"So glad to see you, Miss Ethel," Sylvia's mother said as she took Miss Washington's coat and hat. "How's your mother doing these days?"

"Oh, she's doing fair for an old lady—she keeps me hopping, that's for sure." Miss Washington chuckled. As she shifted her ample weight on the sofa, the plastic creaked.

"Would you like a slice of apple pie and a little tea?" Mrs. Patterson asked, heading to the kitchen even before Miss Washington had a chance to answer.

"You know you make the best pie in the county, Leola. I'd be much obliged."

Mr. Patterson asked his wife for a slice of pie for himself, and spoke to Miss Washington warmly. "So glad to see you, Sister Ethel. So what brings you out on such a cold evening?" he asked as he took a bite of pie.

"Well, I wanted to check on young Gary here, and to tell the truth, I just had a craving for Leola's apple pie, so I figured I would just drop by," Miss Washington replied. *Why is it that grown-ups take a million years to get to their point, when they want us to answer on a dime?*

While the adults laughed, Sylvia squirmed. When they finally got over all the pleasantries, and Miss Washington had eaten two pieces of pie and a slice of cake as well, she looked directly at Gary and said solemnly, "You know they're going to integrate Central High this fall, don't you, son."

"Yes, ma'am. It's about time," Gary replied boldly.

"How do you feel after your unfortunate incident last night? You healing up all right?"

Gary shifted in his seat. "Yes, ma'am. I'm about healed up. Just a little sore. Mama says whatever doesn't kill you makes you stronger. I'll be strong enough to fight again soon."

Sylvia cringed. She knew Gary had no chance with words like that.

"We're looking for bold, brave, nonviolent students, Gary," Miss Washington said gently. "Do you understand what I'm saying?"

Gary looked away from the intensity of her gaze.

Mr. Patterson spoke up. "Integration of the schools won't be happening soon, will it, Sister Ethel? At least not in our lifetime."

Sylvia thought her father sounded hopeful, like she did when she knew the last piece of cake was gone, but she asked for it anyway.

"It's going to take place this year. 1957. September. In your lifetime, and the lives of your children."

Mr. Patterson shook his head. "I'll believe it when I see it."

"The buses were integrated without any trouble last year. We didn't have to do a boycott or anything drastic like they did in Montgomery," Miss Washington offered.

"Yes, I know, but this is not the same," Mr. Patterson said.

"The university is integrated," Miss Washington continued.

"Yes, for a few. We think that's good," Sylvia's mother said. "But I keep remembering the looks of hatred on the faces of Mrs. Crandall and the rest of those white women as those colored students registered for class. You know the old saying,

'If looks could kill' . . ." Mrs. Patterson's voice trailed off and Sylvia rolled her eyes at her sister.

Donna Jean sat next to her, eyes large, hoping, Sylvia knew, that she wouldn't get sent out of the room during this juicy grown-up talk.

"We teachers have been asked to submit names of qualified students to help implement the integration," Miss Washington continued.

"You don't think Gary's name should go on the list?" Sylvia's mother asked, a look of concern and amazement on her face.

"No, not Gary," Miss Washington replied. Gary scowled then looked away.

"You're not suggesting we submit Sylvia Faye to the kind of beating Gary got this week?" Mrs. Patterson asked incredulously.

"There is nothing to indicate that she would be in any physical harm. The school board is grudgingly trying to implement the law of the land." Miss Washington shifted in her seat.

"This is no job for a girl," Sylvia's father said forcefully, "especially my little girl!" Sylvia didn't agree with him about the little girl part, but she was grateful that he wanted to protect her.

"Those women . . ." Sylvia's mother began.

"Are just that. Women with too much time on their hands," Miss Washington said emphatically.

"And malice in their hearts," Sylvia's mother said quietly.

"Sylvia Faye is an excellent student," Miss Washington continued. "I am very proud of not only her academic abilities, but her poise and thoughtfulness as well. She could handle the pressure."

"I don't know, Miss Washington. It's a wonderful honor and opportunity, but it's also potentially very dangerous. Let us think about it for a few days." Mrs. Patterson had started nervously collecting dishes and dusting the spotless coffee table.

"Think about it. Pray about it. Talk about it. Let me know by Monday." Miss Washington got up, and, after thanking Mrs. Patterson for the hospitality, she put on her coat and went on her way. The house suddenly seemed smaller.

Gary was the first to speak. "They should have picked me. I could have protected myself!" He was angry.

"You'd mouth off to some white girl, or smack a white boy, and instead of them tossing a bruised son on my porch, they'd bring you home in a wooden box!" his father told him. Gary twisted his face to respond, but a look from his father made him change his mind.

"What do you think, Sylvia Faye?" her mother asked her quietly. It was the first time all evening anyone had given her a chance to say what was on her mind.

"I like my school," she replied, speaking slowly. "I feel comfortable there. I know everyone, and we all understand each other. It just feels right." Her mother nodded in understanding. "But when I look at Central High School and I see how big and wonderful it is, how much they have and we don't, I don't think it's fair that some law says white kids get to go there, but I can't."

"The only law they understand is fists!" Gary mumbled from his chair.

"Which is why you could never be chosen to do this job,"

his mother told him gently. "This is a time for tolerance and understanding, not violence."

Gary twisted with frustration and glared at his father. "They'll pay attention to violence. We have to fight for our rights."

"There's got to be a better way than fighting," his father reasoned.

"Your way hasn't worked very well the last two hundred years," Gary retorted. "What are you gonna do when they beat Sylvia and she comes home bruised and bloody?" Sylvia felt suddenly chilled.

Mrs. Patterson looked alarmed. DJ ran and buried her head in her mother's lap. "I'm sure that won't happen, Gary," she said as she soothed the trembling child. "The students of Central come from good families like ours. You're just inciting fear."

"What if I'm not?" he asked, his voice a flag of challenge. "Even if she's not physically in danger, how can a flimsy, dreamy girl like her cope with racial slurs, with people hating her?" He turned to Sylvia. "You need for people to like you, don't you, Sylvie?"

"Well, sure. But I'm stronger than you think, Gary," Sylvia told him.

"No, you're not. Remember last year when that group of girls at school decided you were too smart? They made fun of you, picked on you, and refused to invite you to their parties. You came home in tears more than once."

"That was different," Sylvia insisted. But she looked at the floor instead of Gary.

"What if these people make you cry, Sylvie?" Gary said in a gentle voice. "I hate to see you cry."

Sylvia walked over to her brother and gave him a hug. "Thanks, Gary Berry," she whispered into his shoulder, using the nickname she'd given him when she was four.

"I won't allow you to be threatened or hurt, Sylvia Faye," her father said with feeling. He stood up and stretched, but his face was lined with tension. "I refuse to risk your safety."

"We don't have to decide anything now, Daddy," Sylvia found herself saying, even though she wasn't completely sure she wanted to do this. "Even if my name goes on the list, that doesn't mean I'll be chosen. We have lots of time to think about it and decide later."

"Miss Ethel doesn't give recommendations like that lightly," her mother said.

"And she doesn't usually make house calls, either!" Her father chuckled.

"So is Sylvia Faye going to go to Central High in the fall?" Donna Jean piped up.

"Maybe," their mother replied slowly. "Maybe."

Her father, as he placed his large hand on Sylvia's shoulder, said to her then, "I'm really proud of you, Sylvie. You're a gift to us all." Sylvia glanced at her brother, but he had turned to tickle DJ.

Her mother blinked back tears. Sylvia wasn't sure if it was pride or fear she saw in her mother's eyes.

Wednesday, January 9, 1957

I just got finished looking at myself closely—at least as much of me as I can see in our tiny bathroom mirror.

The mirror is a little warped, but it showed me a brown-skinned girl with puffy black hair, a nose that's too large for her face, and full, possibly kissable lips, assuming I could find somebody who wanted to kiss them. Reggie's lips would be a nice starting point!

I have ridiculously bushy eyebrows and short, stubby eyelashes. Okay, I'll never be a movie star. My skin is too oily, so my face always looks shiny—I hate that—and I have tiny little pimples that dot my forehead and cheeks. Goodness! I'll never get married at this rate!

Looking at myself on the inside is even harder. I'm not talking about hearts and lungs and stuff like that, but whether I'm brave like Miss Washington said, or noble, or admirable, or any of those adjectives they only use at somebody's funeral. I know I'm just as intelligent as any white student, and just as worthy of a good education as anybody else in this country. Why should the color of my skin make a difference? I don't get it.

When I was about six, I went with Mama the only time she ever did housecleaning for Mrs. Crandall. Mama didn't like doing day work, but we needed the extra money. I remember she hesitated before going into the Crandalls' house.

Mama moved stiffly and kept her jaws tight as Mrs. Crandall, dressed in pearls and a tailored dress, like a lady in a *Life* magazine ad, demanded that Mama clean the dusty corners of her house, which was not nearly as nice as ours. Callie Crandall, the same age as me, followed her mother around, tossing her long blond hair as she stuck her tongue out at me.

When Callie sat down on the sofa next to me, I reached out and touched her hair, out of curiosity. It felt a little like curly silk. Then she reached over and touched my hair. She said it felt nasty like monkey hair. I got up from the couch and stayed close to my mother. We never went back to that house.

Is that what it would be like if I went to Central? Will it be full of kids who think the darkness of my skin will run off and dirty them? The thought makes me feel sick. But I'm sure there would be nice kids there, too, like Rachel. Everything is so complicated.

My parents watch my every move and try to control my thoughts as well. How am I supposed to learn how to be an adult if I don't even get the chance to figure out stuff by myself? I think it's time I *do* something!

SUNDAY, JANUARY 13, 1957

Hallelujah, Church!" Pastor Patterson intoned from the pulpit. "I've got a special message for you today, my brothers and sisters. But first, join me in a chorus or two of 'Shelter in the Time of Storm.'" In his rich tenor voice Sylvia's father began, and the church joined him as he sang:

"My Lord is a rock in a weary land, weary land, weary land
My Lord is a rock in a weary land
Shelter in the time of the storm . . ."

Sylvia loved old hymns like this one. The minor key and the sadness behind the words made her shiver. It was cool to know that same song had given strength to people a long time ago.

As the last notes of the hymn filtered up to the highest ceiling of the church, perhaps even to Heaven, the room was stilled, waiting, strangely expectant. The small auditorium carried the faint fragrance of the roses in Miss Lillie's bouquets, mixed with the usual comforting Sunday smells of floor wax and burning candles and Old Spice cologne.

Though she would never want her father to know, this was the time in the service Sylvia usually spent daydreaming. His sermons weren't exactly exciting. She wondered mildly what today's "special message" would be. She noticed that Reggie, sitting just one pew over, also seemed more attentive than usual.

Pastor Patterson raised his arms in the air, as if he was reaching out to Heaven, and began to speak. "You know, my daddy used to tell me, 'Son, times are a-changin'. You better get on that train to glory, because I can see the handwriting on the wall!' Of course, his statement didn't make much sense to me as a child. Old folks are famous for mixing metaphors—forgive him."

The congregation chuckled.

"But my daddy had a vision of the future that I couldn't see at the time. I lost my father when I was a very young man—he was killed because of hatred and bigotry, and I lost his vision when I lost him."

He paused and wiped his brow.

"Yes, my terrible loss made me close my eyes to reality. I've been afraid to face the future, afraid to offer my children—Gary, Sylvia Faye, and Donna Jean—any hope of getting on that train." The rows of people shifted like water as everyone turned to look at them.

Sylvia blushed deeply. Her father never talked about family. He believed some things ought to be private, and Sylvia had always appreciated that.

Donna Jean, sitting next to Sylvia, wore patent-leather shoes, lacy socks, and a starched yellow dress. She leaned over and whispered with pride, "He's talking about us!"

"*Sh-sh-sh,*" their mother admonished.

Pastor Patterson's voice rose. "Our rock, Little Rock, truly is a rock in a weary land, friends. Let me hear you say 'Amen' if you're weary!"

"Amen!" the congregation cried out with feeling.

"Let me hear you say 'Amen' if you feel like you need a rock in a weary land!"

"Amen!" they called out.

"Let me hear you say 'Amen!' if you need shelter in the time of the storm!"

For a third time they all repeated, "Amen! Amen!"

When the church had quieted, Pastor Patterson continued. "They're talking about integrating the schools of Little Rock. It's been a rumor for years, but this year it looks as though it will really happen. They want to take your children and my children and let these young people do what we can't—change the world."

"Here it comes," Sylvia leaned over and whispered to DJ. "He's gonna stomp all over the idea." Their mother shushed them both with a touch of her gloved hand.

Pastor Patterson paused. "I think we ought to let them try."

While murmurs broke out all around her, Sylvia sat stunned.

"My son is an angry young man, as I once was," the pastor continued. The murmurs stopped suddenly, as if everyone had suddenly inhaled.

"He wants to change the world this very instant, and he's been physically attacked as a result." Sylvia turned to observe Gary, who was sitting on the very back pew. He was staring at his father with astonishment.

"Of my two daughters, my baby girl, Donna Jean, is already a victim of hatred at age eight, and my older daughter, Sylvia, often looks at me with eyes of disappointment and despair. Unless she needs lunch money," he added. The church needed the levity.

I didn't think he knew how I felt, Sylvia thought with amazement. Her father always seemed so distant. He'd tell her what to do, but he never really talked with her.

Sylvia glanced over to where Reggie was sitting. Dressed in a black suit that was a little too small and a skinny red tie, he grinned at her, then turned his attention back to her father. She noticed that he wore shiny black shoes instead of his favorite tennis shoes.

"They've asked me to let Sylvia Faye be on the list of students who might be considered to integrate Central High School," her father told the church. "I know that some of you have been approached as well. I can't think of anything more terrifying than sending my little girl into danger, but I'm inclined to let her try."

Sylvia gasped. Her mother reached over and squeezed Sylvia's hand. Even through the thickness of her mother's white gloves, the tingle of her touch made Sylvia squeeze back. *Just when you think you've got your parents all figured out, they turn around and act like humans.*

Pastor Patterson opened the huge Bible in front of him. "If

you look in the book of Judges, you'll find the story of Gideon—
a brave young man, but not the strongest kid in the neighborhood. He tells the Lord that he comes from the weakest tribe
and that he's the feeblest of them all. Like the Lord didn't
already know that!"

The congregation chuckled while they searched for the
passage.

"But the Lord told Gideon, 'I'm gonna be with you, son.
Don't be afraid. You ain't gonna die—at least not today.'" He
wiped his brow.

"Friends, I've been afraid all my life. Maybe it's time for me
to step out on faith."

Sylvia gazed at her father with wonder. Surely someone had
taken her father away and replaced him with this man who
looked just like him.

"You know, we humans tend to need proof, even when
it's the Lord who is making the promises. We're pretty weak
when it comes to faith. To prove to Gideon that he had no
need to be afraid, the Lord made fire explode from a rock—it
burned up everything that had been on the stone. Can you just
picture it?"

Sylvia glanced over at Reggie again. He mouthed the word
"Whoosh!" and acted like he was using a fire hose. His mother
smacked him on the back of his head and told him to be still.
He just rolled his eyes and smiled at Sylvia once more.

"What I'm trying to say, Church, is maybe we need to look
around and make some hard decisions. I guess all that fire
made Gideon a believer. Because you know what? In the battle
the next day, the Lord gave him the victory!"

Pastor Patterson kept preaching for another few minutes, but Sylvia didn't hear much of it. She was too overwhelmed with her father's sudden turnaround and the now very real prospect of her name going on the list.

After church, lots of people came up to Sylvia, giving her words of encouragement or suggestions. Sister Hortense, the oldest member, hobbled over to her, leaning heavily on her cane. She used that cane as a weapon sometimes, bopping children on the head when they talked too much during service. Kids learned early to keep out of her way. She said, "Chile, you been chosen for a very special task. The Lord will bless you for it." Sylvia thanked her, glad she was in a good mood.

Not everyone, however, was so supportive. One woman, whose rolls of fat under her tight white suit made her look like yeast bread in the bowl, waddled over to Sylvia and said, "Stick with your own kind, girl. Mixing the races will only get you hurt. They don't want you there. You hear?"

"Yes, ma'am," Sylvia replied politely.

Another lady, Sister Simpson, wearing very high heels, tiptoed over to Sylvia and whispered in her ear, "The colored schools were good enough for me, and good enough for your parents as well. Don't try to get uppity, little girl."

Again Sylvia knew nothing else to say but "Yes, ma'am."

Lillie Cobbs, however, who was dressed in a pale green wool suit, pushed the other woman aside and told Sylvia, "Don't pay her no mind, child. She don't know nothin' about progress. If you feel like you can do this, the Lord will protect you from small-minded people from both races!" Sylvia could smell gardenias in her reassuring hug.

Sylvia noticed Reggie standing near the edge of a group of teenaged boys. All too cool to wear winter coats, Sylvia could tell they were trying not to shiver in their crisp white shirts. They all laughed a little too loudly as Calvin purposely slipped on a piece of ice, showing off for the teenaged girls who stood in another small group, their full skirts billowing under their woolen coats. The girls, hair tightly curled and slick with pomade, giggled together, and whispered about the boys. None of them, as far as Sylvia knew, had been selected to go on the list. Already she was starting to feel left out.

Sylvia stood alone near the front steps. The two groups of teens broke up as parents called their children to load into their cars, but instead of heading to the parking lot, Reggie walked right up to Sylvia. She held her breath and pretended to act casual.

"Hey, Big Shot," he teased.

"Hi, Reggie."

"Are you scared?"

"A little."

"Are you sure you want to do this?" he asked. "I don't think it's a very good idea."

"Why?"

"White folks."

"Huh?"

"You'll stick out like a raisin in a bowl of rice."

Sylvia smiled at the thought, then looked down at her shoes. "I know," she said with a sigh.

"You got guts, Sylvia Faye. And you got class. But I don't know if you've got good sense."

She looked at him quizzically. "How can you compliment me and insult me in the same sentence?"

He ignored her question. "And you're really pretty, you know," he said quietly.

Sylvia felt hot despite the chilly wind. "Thanks," she managed to say as she thought, *He's looking at me like I'm a piece of chocolate cake.*

"You know, there's one thing you might want to consider as you figure out what to do about September," Reggie added casually. He leaned against a tree and pulled off a brittle twig, showing no sign of nervousness at all.

"What's that?"

"Well, I'll be at Horace Mann with the rest of the colored kids. And you'll be at Central." He picked a tooth with the end of the twig.

"Yes, so?" Sylvia's heart thudded.

"I'd like my girlfriend to be at the same school with me. Dances. Games. Movies. Who will I take if you're not there?"

Sylvia didn't know how to act like this was no big deal. She wondered what Lou Ann would say. When she finally found her voice, Sylvia said, with as much feminine coyness as she could find, "Who says I'm your girlfriend?" She smiled tightly, trying to hold back all the fizz she felt inside.

"*I* do." He turned then and headed to his mother's car. "I'll call you. See you at school tomorrow." Reggie said casually. "And don't forget we've got a date next Friday!" he called back.

"Sure," she replied, as if this happened every day. She felt like dancing in the snow.

Monday, January 14, 1957

Yesterday the telephone rang constantly. Some calls were from other parents whose children are being considered as possible candidates for Central, but many were from friends and family with differing opinions. There were a couple of calls from Miss Daisy Bates, the president of the Arkansas NAACP. Everybody knows her—she lives not far from us on W. 28th Street. I think she's pretty—and such a proud, powerful lady. Daddy says she's pushy. That's probably true, too. Gary thinks that Miss Daisy and her husband, L.C., who publish our local Negro newspaper, are heroes.

Lou Ann called just before supper and told me to wear something red to the game. She said if I show up in beige or brown, she would bop me on the head with a saddle oxford! Reggie finally called just before supper. We didn't talk long, but it seemed like every word was glowing with importance. What's funny is I've known Reggie practically all my life, but all of a sudden he makes my stomach feel like mashed potatoes.

I still haven't gotten used to the idea that we're together, and he asked me again what it will be like when we're apart in the fall. I told him it may not happen and it's so far away I'm not going to worry about it yet. But the truth is, I am worried.

Gary is grumpy and irritable. He's like a balloon that's been blown up too far—all he needs is the pin that will make him pop. He wants to be on the list so bad he can taste it. I'm on the list, but I'm afraid to swallow. I wish I could trade places with him.

Miss Washington seemed very pleased when I handed her Mama's letter, giving permission for me to be considered. Several other students from Dunbar and Horace Mann had also been asked, including, I found out, my friend Melba Patillo.

Since our last names both start with "P," Melba and I usually ended up sitting near each other when she went to Dunbar last year. She liked to read as much as I do, and we often shared library books. Plus she can sew like no tomorrow. Once, when I admired a skirt she wore, she brought me the pattern the next day. She'll be a great choice to be one of the students to integrate the school.

Even though me and DJ cleaned up the kitchen, I can hear Mama downstairs going behind us, sweeping and wiping the places we missed, softly singing one of her "worry songs," as she calls them. She has a lovely voice—deep and mellow—and I feel safe when I hear it. Sometimes she just hums, but every once in a while, she really belts it out. I bet she could have been a professional singer if she hadn't married Daddy and had us.

I've read about Marian Anderson, the first colored lady to sing at the Metropolitan Opera. She even sang on the steps of the Lincoln Memorial in Washington, D.C. I wonder if the opera folks treated her like she was special, or if they made her go in the back door like Aunt Bessie had to do for Mr. Crandall's shirts. I hope not. I'd love to hear her sing, just to compare her voice to Mama's, but colored folks hardly ever show up on television, and if she sang on the radio, I missed it.

TUESDAY, JANUARY 15, 1957

I need you to go to the Zuckers' grocery, Sylvie, to pick up a few things for supper. And can you get a little bouquet from Miss Lillie's? Just some carnations. I want the dinner table to look nice. Can you do that for me?" her mother called out.

"Sure! I'll be right down." Sylvia grabbed a jacket and a scarf for her head and headed down the steps. She wondered what Rachel would say when she heard Sylvia's big news—both school stuff and boy stuff. Actually, she knew that Rachel would be thrilled. Rachel, of course, went to the junior high for white students, but in spite of the distance that society had placed between them, they remained friends.

The store, only a couple of blocks away from her house, was popular with neighborhood folks of both races. Parents would often wrap a few coins in a piece of paper and send their child on a hurried mission with a note to Mrs. Zucker to send a pound of sugar or a can of baking powder. She'd wrap it carefully and send the child back home with the correct change and sometimes a warm chocolate chip cookie.

Mr. Crandall's barbershop, two doors down from the Zuckers' store, wasn't as inviting. He cut the hair of white men only, although he'd refused to cut Mr. Zucker's hair the one time he'd walked into Crandall's shop. The two men rarely spoke. None of the colored men in town wanted Crandall to touch their hair—even if he would. They all went to Zeke's place, where gossip and gospel music buzzed all day along with the razors.

Miss Lillie's tiny flower shop, which had fresh decorations in the window each day, smelled of honeysuckle today. Sylvia inhaled deeply of the rich fragrance as she entered.

"Good afternoon, Miss Lillie," Sylvia said to the woman dressed in green work shoes and dark green smock. Miss Lillie wore a red scarf on her fuzzy hair, so from a distance she really did look like an odd flower in bloom.

"How's your mama?" Miss Lillie asked as she clipped petals on a bouquet in front of her.

"She's good. She sends you her best," Sylvia replied politely. "She wants a small bouquet of carnations."

"I got some pink ones right here," Miss Lillie said as she deftly wrapped a bow around the flowers. You celebratin' at your house tonight?"

"Not exactly. Mama just likes to make things special at dinner. Things have been so ugly lately, and a few flowers can go a long way to make life seem prettier."

Miss Lillie wiped a speck of dirt from her face. "I agree completely. You know, Sylvie, you've been chosen to do something special in the world. It might be this integration stuff, it might be something else. But I see something in you that I don't see in other teenagers, not even in my own Calvin, bless his heart. He's a good boy, but he won't change the world. You will." She turned her gaze back to the bouquet. Sylvia couldn't understand what grown-ups thought they saw in her. She sure didn't see anything special.

"Uh, thanks," Sylvia said uncomfortably as she paid for the flowers. She didn't know what else to say. "Tell Calvin I'll see him at school tomorrow."

"Sure thing. And can you take this bouquet to Mrs. Zucker?" Miss Lillie asked Sylvia. "She loves red roses." Sylvia nodded, took both bouquets, and hurried out of the flower shop and into the Zuckers' store.

With well-polished hardwood floors and shelves from floor to ceiling, Zucker's store carried everything from peanuts to peppercorns, from candles to batteries. The door had a little bell on it that jingled when a customer entered. Sylvia loved the smell of the store—like wax and pickles and maple syrup. And on the days like today when Mrs. Zucker baked, it smelled like cinnamon and vanilla as well.

Rachel was sitting in the middle of an aisle with a box of Argo starch in one hand and Clabber Girl baking powder in the other, helping her father stock the shelves.

Like the gentleman he was, Mr. Zucker stood up stiffly and shook Sylvia's hand. "Always a pleasure to see you, my child," he said warmly in his thick German accent. He wore, as usual, a long-sleeved white shirt. Sylvia could tell it had been through many washings—the buttons were yellowed.

"You look well, Mr. Zucker, and I'm glad to see you're finally making Rachel do some work around here!" Sylvia said with a laugh.

"Ach! Her young mind runs circles around me. Already she has begun to rearrange the shelves. Soon I won't be able to find anything in my own store! I'll leave you two to chat. I must see if Mrs. Z's latest cake creation is out of the oven yet." He chuckled and walked to the back room.

"Papa exaggerates," Rachel said, smiling. "He's trying to teach me the business, but his shelving system makes no sense! How've you been, Sylvia Faye? It is *so* good to see you!" She stood up and gave Sylvia a big hug.

"So what are you up to, besides ruining your father's store?" Sylvia asked, plopping comfortably on the floor, setting the flowers carefully next to her.

"Well, to be perfectly honest, Papa is really old-fashioned, so my brother Ruben will probably run the business end of the store, but I think girls ought to know how to do that kind of thing as well. Don't you agree?" She shook her head good-naturedly.

Sylvia thought about the women she'd seen in those magazine ads—all of them housewives, not professionals. "Absolutely," she said. "I want to do more than what I see women doing on television, Rachel," Sylvia admitted. "*I Love Lucy* is a great show, but all she does is stay home, clean house, and get in trouble with Ricky! Besides, who's gonna take seriously a lady who's wearing a lace apron and holding a mixing spoon in her hand?"

Both girls laughed. "That's why Lucy is so popular! You and I think alike, Sylvia Faye. Do you think there will ever be a television program with a policewoman or lady detective or lady doctor as the main character?"

"Only if she's funny and acts silly," Sylvia replied as she helped Rachel sort the goods for the shelves. "So what else is new in your life?"

"Oh, you know, school, boys, homework, and collecting Elvis Presley records! Can you believe they're going to send him to the army? What a waste!" She tossed her dark hair, which she wore in a long, curled ponytail. "What about you?"

"Well, I'm more of a Platters than a Presley fan," Sylvia told her, "but I spend a lot of time playing with my little sister, helping my mother around the house, and doing loads and loads of homework." Sylvia really loved her family and how they lived, but describing it to someone else made it seem boring and insignificant. "Whatever happened to that boy named Mario who called you?" she asked her friend.

Rachel had an infectious laugh. "Oh, he was way too Italian and way too Catholic for my old-fashioned parents. Remember when we talked about that at your house? I would have dated him anyway, but it turns out he had rotten teeth and unbelievably bad breath! I had to let him go."

Both girls doubled over with amusement. Mrs. Zucker ambled over to where the girls sat, a plate of warm chocolate cake in each hand. "Greetings, Sylvia. What makes you girls so full of life today?"

"Boys, Mama," Rachel said, teasing her mother. "Horrible, wonderful boys!"

"Ah, Sylvia," Mrs. Zucker said, smiling and shaking her head as she gave the cake to the girls. "Can you teach my Rachel some social graces?" She touched her daughter 's hair.

"Thanks for the yummy chocolate, Mrs. Zucker, but she's never listened to me before. I think she's a lost cause!" Sylvia replied with a chuckle. "Oh, and Miss Lillie asked me to give you these roses."

Mrs. Zucker took the flowers as if they were jewels. "Such beauty! Ah, such a sweet woman is Miss Lillie. I must take her a slice of cake."

"Chocolate is her favorite," Sylvia said.

Mrs. Zucker sniffed the roses with pleasure. "How is your mother, Sylvia?"

"She's fine. She said to send you her best."

"Before you leave, I will wrap several slices of cake for you to take. Gary and Donna Jean love my chocolate cake!"

"Thank you, ma'am. You're very kind." Sylvia knew not to refuse the gift. It would be an insult.

"Did you save an extra piece for me?" Mr. Zucker asked as he joined them. His plate was empty except for the crumbs.

Sylvia noticed he'd rolled up the sleeves of his shirt. The numbers on his arm seemed to shout as she looked away, pretending she hadn't noticed. How awful to be reminded every single day of something horrible that happened in your past. When she glanced back, he was rolling down and buttoning his shirtsleeves.

"Look in the back room, love," his wife said, covering the momentary embarrassment. "On the top shelf. Where I always hide your second piece." She looked at the girls closely. "Those boys you two laugh about grow up to be men. Be careful how you choose. Find a man who cares about who you are inside, rather than what you look like."

She walked away then, still sniffing the roses, to the cash register to wait on another customer.

"Your mother makes a lot of sense," Sylvia said thoughtfully. "Speaking of boys, you know that Reggie Birmingham I told you about?"

"Yeah?"

"He calls me almost every night, he sits with me at lunch, and we're going to a basketball game on Friday!"

Rachel squealed with delight. "A real date! How peachy keen! How did you get your mother to agree? More important, what are you gonna wear?"

Sylvia scratched her head. "I hadn't really thought about it yet, but my friend Lou Ann says it should be something red. And it's not an official date, since he's too young to drive. I'm just meeting him at the game and we're going to sit together."

"That counts as a real date in my book!" Rachel stood up, stretched, and twirled around in excitement.

"All of a sudden I've gone from Sylvia the old maid to Sylvia the girlfriend. It's kinda hard to get used to," Sylvia admitted.

"So you're complaining?" Rachel asked with a giggle as she plopped back down.

Sylvia grinned. "Not likely! He's like taking a new subject in school—with lots of homework to figure it all out."

"Now that's the kind of homework I like!" Rachel replied as she placed another can on the shelf. "A course in the anatomy and physiology of the teenage male!"

Sylvia felt herself blush. "Girl, stop."

Rachel stood up and picked up both plates and forks. "I can't wait to get out of ninth grade and go to Central in the fall! That's where all the cute boys are!" she added enthusiastically. She was suddenly quiet then, realizing she had entered a danger zone.

"I may go to Central, too," Sylvia told her casually. She knew she probably shouldn't have said anything yet, since nothing was even close to official, but she just had to tell Rachel.

"Really? That's neat," Rachel said, a little too enthusiastically. Neither of them said anything for a moment. "Seriously, Sylvia Faye," Rachel said finally. "I don't know if I could do what you might have to do. But know this—you will always have a friend at Central High School."

Sylvia embraced Rachel again and thanked her. Then she quickly found the items her mother had asked her to pick up, and hurried home, carrying soup, flour, salt, a bouquet of flowers, half a cake, and the memory of a genuine hug from her friend.

Thursday, January 17, 1957
Miss Washington didn't waste any time assigning our research papers for this semester, so I'm glad I didn't bring her that last piece of Mrs. Zucker's cake. I decided to give it to Reggie instead. He loved it, of

course, and licked the waxed paper it had been wrapped in. Miss Washington is big enough—she doesn't need more baked goods!

I don't know why teachers make kids do homework like this—I guess she has nothing better to do than read stacks of student papers. She says the process is supposed to teach us something. Well, I've certainly learned something, but it wasn't what I expected.

Last year Daddy bought a set of World Book encyclopedias from a door-to-door salesman who was a friend of Mr. Zucker. I know it's sometimes a squeeze for Daddy to make the weekly payments on the books, but he believes that education is the key to success. Maybe it will be for me and Donna Jean. I worry about Gary though. I can't see him sitting still long enough to get through college.

I curled up on the sofa with the volume *N* on my lap. I love the smell of a new book. The maroon binding was still tight and almost squeaked as I opened it to reveal thousands of pages of small print and really neat photos. I wanted to look up information on the Negro for my research paper. I saw a picture of Napoleon, looking surprisingly baby-faced, articles on navigation and nature, and a map of Nebraska.

Finally I came to the article entitled "*Negro.*" I was excited at first, but then I couldn't believe what I was seeing! First I looked at the pictures—a frowning little brown boy, obviously on a farm, holding a basket of vegetables. Jackie Robinson—the first Negro to play major league baseball. A dentist, with a caption below that said, "A Negro dentist in a well-equipped office treats a patient of his own race." A smiling Pullman porter in uniform, with the caption "Pullman porters are known in all parts of the United Stated for their smiling courtesy and efficient service on trains." I felt a funny pang in my stomach.

As I continued to read the article, I felt downright sick. Words started jumping off the page and slapping me in my face. I wrote them down so I could copy them in my diary. "Such Negroid physical traits as dark skin, kinky hair, and long arms . . . ," and "Negroes as well as whites have generally disapproved of intermarriage of the two groups," and "Social conditions for the Negroes are gradually improving, but many still live under slum conditions in overcrowded houses without bathrooms, running water, electric lights, or refrigerators." In a million years when somebody finds this diary, they won't believe that such mean stuff could be printed in America in 1957.

Yes, the article mentioned the accomplishments of Negroes like Harry Belafonte and Ralph Bunche and George Washington Carver, but it was obviously written by a white person who was describing my people the same way I would do a report on bugs! "In recent years, some progress has been made in improving the life of the African Negro, but his position is still far from desirable."

If I need to know about frogs or stars or blood vessels, I'll know where to look. But for information about Negroes, I've got to look elsewhere. I wonder if the textbooks at Central High are all like this.

TUESDAY, JANUARY 22, 1957

So, when will I start going to school with white children?" Donna Jean asked as she and Sylvia got ready for bed.

Sylvia, wrapping her hair onto brown paper rollers, looked at her sister with surprise. "Do you really want to, DJ?"

"No, I don't—that's the point. I like my school. I just want to know how long I have before grown-ups mess everything up." She was glancing through the pages of one of their mother's *Life* magazines.

"I don't think you have anything to worry about for a while," Sylvia told her with a smile. "Adults who change laws work unbelievably slow."

"That's good to know. My friend Vanessa says white people rule the whole world, that they control everything and everybody. Is that true?"

"Well, sort of, I guess. But that doesn't mean it's right, or that it will last forever."

Donna Jean brushed her hair while she talked. "When we watched the inauguration tonight, I was wondering what you have to do to become president. Eisenhower doesn't look so special to me—just another bald-headed white man in a nice suit."

"You're pretty deep, kid," Sylvia said with genuine admiration. "I think the requirement is to be able to give long, boring speeches!"

"Then Daddy can be president for sure!" Donna Jean said with a grin. "Except he's colored." She stopped smiling. "Look at this," she said then, still looking at the magazine. "The new 'Miss America TV.'"

Sylvia glanced down at the page. Miss America stood there next to the television set with her shimmering gold crown, blond hair, and lovely flowing gown. Both girls simply sighed. "Wow."

Donna Jean said, "Miss America looks so beautiful—like one of those fairy princesses in my storybooks at school."

"None of that stuff is real, Donna Jean," Sylvia reminded her.

"I know that. But Miss America is real, isn't she?"

Sylvia sighed and shook her head. "She may as well be a fairy tale, as far as we're concerned."

Donna Jean asked, "Don't you ever think about growing up to be Miss America?"

Sylvia laughed. "Not likely, little sister."

"Why not?" Donna Faye continued. "You're pretty."

Sylvia looked at her, surprised. "There's no way they'd ever let a Negro be Miss America," she told her sister. "Never in a million years."

Gary popped his head in the door then. "Hey, Miss Roller-Head," he said, teasing Sylvia.

"Hey, yourself."

"Shouldn't midgets be asleep by now?" he asked DJ, walking over to her bed and tickling her. She giggled and hid under the covers.

"So, you ready to become a freedom fighter?" Gary asked Sylvia casually.

"You'd be much better at this than me, Gary," she told him honestly.

He sighed. "I know. But you've got the brains and the personality to make it work. I'd end up burning the place down."

"Or getting burned up yourself," Sylvia added.

"I'm a little scared for you, little sis," he said gently.

"Are you sure this is the right thing to do?" she asked him. "It would be so much easier to stay with my friends and go on to Horace Mann, and only have to worry about whether Reggie likes my new dress."

"Don't worry," Gary said, laughing. "I've seen how Reggie

acts around you. At the game Friday he was acting like a puppy with a new toy."

"You could tell?" Sylvia asked, blushing a little.

"Oh, yeah! You've got that one tied up!" Gary replied with a grin.

Donna Jean poked her head out from under the covers and chanted in a singsong voice, "Sylvie and Reggie, sitting in a tree, K-I-S-S-I-N-G!" She repeated the rhyme several times until Gary started tickling her again.

When she quieted down, Sylvia said, "Reggie says it's cool I got picked, but I know he wants me to stay at Mann. He's sending me mixed messages."

"That's because both sides of this issue are so strong. Either way, you'll win and you'll lose. No matter what happens."

"I'm all mixed up, Gary."

"Well, since it looks like it's not gonna be me, I can't think of anyone better than you to do this," Gary said as he leaned over and kissed her on the forehead. "I'm proud of you, Sylvie."

Sylvia's eyes filled with tears as Gary gently closed her door.

Tuesday, January 22, 1957

When Donna Jean told me she thought I was pretty, I was really shocked. First of all, she had never given me a compliment before— most of the time we tease each other, using names like "hunchback" and "beady ball." But more than that, I have never in my life thought of myself as pretty. I guess I'm fair looking, maybe, but certainly not pretty. I don't even know what the definition of pretty is. Is it what I see in the mirror, or what I see in Mama's magazines? And what does Reggie see? That is, if he's still looking at me.

In *Life* magazine, like DJ said, all the women in the ads are white. They have pale skin and silky hair and they look sophisticated and in control. But is that what makes them attractive? Is it the blond hair? That couldn't be, because many of them have hair as black as mine, and red hair, and brown, and every other combination as well. So is it their small lips? Their tiny noses? I've got full lips and a large nose. Does that make me ugly? I have no idea.

Reggie seems to think I look okay, but I know he thinks Candy looks better. Where did she get those hips and those D-cups? I can't compete with equipment like that. Most of the boys at school, including Reggie, are attracted to Candy Castle like bees to honey, but it's not just because of her body. She has some other quality that makes them hover around her all the time. I don't know what it is, and I don't know how to get it.

In *Ebony* magazine, most of the women in the ads are Negro, but very few of them have dark skin like mine. Actually, most of them look more like the white women in *Life* magazine than they look like me. I wonder what colored men think of those models. What about white men? What attracts them? Does race make a difference? And how does all this fit in with the integration stuff?

When I was little I had a doll called Tiny Tears. I never gave her a real name—I simply called her Tiny. I loved that doll more than life. I still have her, and every once in a while I go to the top of my closet, get her out of the box I keep her in, and unwrap her carefully. I keep her wrapped in one of Donna Jean's old baby blankets. When I take Tiny Tears out and hold her in my arms, the smell of her, almost like baby powder, still makes me smile. Her eyes really blink in her sculpted face.

When you squeeze the doll's tummy, she coos. That sound, the feel of her soft, rubber body, even her slightly scratched, painted-on hair take me back to a time of safety and happiness and real joy. I still love that doll and she is the most beautiful thing I own. And she's a little white baby. They don't make Negro dolls.

WEDNESDAY JANUARY 30, 1957

Hi, Reggie." Sylvia flopped down on the floor and twisted the long black telephone cord in her fingers. She still couldn't get used to him calling every day, but she sure didn't want it to stop!

"Hey, Sylvie. Let me ask you something—do you think snowballs fly farther when the weather is colder?"

Sylvia laughed. "You're silly. When I throw them, they just kinda land not far from my feet."

"Sounds like I need to give you throwing lessons," Reggie said softly on the other end of the line. "I'll put my arms around you, then take your arm in my hand, and help you toss that snowball to the next county!"

Sylvia gasped, but managed to say in a squeak, "I just might let you do that!" Most of the time Reggie didn't make her feel nervous at all anymore. She used to feel sweaty, but gradually she had relaxed enough to talk to him without feeling like she couldn't swallow. But he always managed to say something that curled her socks!

Reggie laughed, deep and throaty. Then, his voice turning serious, he asked, "Did you hear about the bombing of Dr.

King's house down in Alabama? I told you white folks were hateful and dangerous."

"That's not fair, Reggie. Not all white people are like that." Sylvia frowned. "My friend Rachel is open and understanding and really pretty cool about all this stuff."

"Does she have a brother?"

"Huh?"

"If you wanted to marry her brother, what would her daddy say? Would he welcome you into the family? Would she?"

"Her brother is a nerd—there's no way I'd marry him!" Sylvia tried to laugh it off, but she knew what Reggie was talking about.

"Don't get fooled by what you think is friendship, Sylvie. Lions hang with lions. Bears hang with bears. They don't mix."

"I think you're being mean and unfair!" But she felt uncomfortable, because there was some truth in his words.

"So, what did your father think about the bombing?" Reggie asked.

Sylvia shifted in her seat. "I heard Daddy talking about it with some of the other ministers last night," she told Reggie. "He was really upset."

"Did he sound scared?"

"No. Surprisingly, Daddy was angry. I've never seen him like that—mad enough to *do* something!"

"Tell your daddy to call me if he ever decides to get up off his knees and get out into the streets where the real action is," Reggie said with feeling.

"Reggie!" Sylvia replied, a little surprised at his outburst.

"I'm sorry. I don't mean no disrespect to your daddy, but

everybody in his generation wants to sit around and wait for things to get better—my folks included. It's time to get up and do something."

"You sound like Gary."

"Gary's cool. He understands. You know, if men like Martin Luther King, or even girls like you, are going to try to change the world, it's not going to happen quietly," Reggie told Sylvia.

"I know. I bet Dr. King was terrified when that bomb woke him up. He has little kids," Sylvia added. Her right ear was getting sweaty, so she switched to the left.

"I wonder if something like that could happen here in Little Rock," Reggie mused. "People are getting awfully riled up about the school integration."

"I sure hope not," Sylvia replied, imagining what it would be like to have a bomb detonate on her porch. She shuddered.

"If somebody ever tried to mess with you, Sylvie, I'd hurt 'em bad. Real bad," Reggie said boldly.

"That's probably the sweetest thing anybody has ever said to me," Sylvia said softly. "Also the dumbest. You're not Superman, Reggie."

"Neither are you." He paused. "You know, Sylvie, I know I have no right to tell you what to do, but I've thought about this quite a bit, and I don't want you to go to Central. I want you to go to high school and just be normal, not some kind of hero."

"Oh, Reggie! I don't know what to say." Sylvia felt tears welling up.

"I just want you to be with me. Is that too much to ask?"

Sylvia sighed. "Please don't make this harder than it is.

This whole thing is bigger than both of us, Reggie." The phone lines were silent as neither of them spoke for a moment. "Do you think white folks imagine the same world we do?" she asked quietly.

"Probably not."

"Do you think they're scared like we are?" Sylvia asked thoughtfully.

"I ain't scared of nobody!"

"Hey, my mother is calling me. I have to get off the phone now."

Just as he had the last few times they'd talked on the telephone, Reggie said softly, "See you later, alligator."

Sylvia tried to cover the excitement she felt, and she knew it was corny, but she loved the fact that she had a stupid little custom that involved a boy. She said calmly in reply, "After while, crocodile." She hung up the phone, a slight smile on her face, a faint frown behind it.

Wednesday January 30, 1957

My father is no Martin Luther King. He's old and set in his ways, or in ways that have been set for him. I'm pretty sure a bomb on our front porch would send him running to Alaska, not to the NAACP office to become a freedom fighter.

Daddy has met Rev. King a couple of times at church-related activities. I know he admires Dr. King for the work he's doing in Alabama, but I'm glad my father comes home every night and we don't get bombs tossed on our porch. It's bad enough I get brothers tossed at our front door.

When Miss Rosa Parks got arrested a couple of years ago because she refused to give up her bus seat to a white woman, it was Dr. King who helped the Negroes in Montgomery organize a boycott. For a whole year they walked everywhere they had to go until they won the right to sit anywhere they wanted to on the public buses.

I was a little surprised when *Life* magazine ran a story on the boycotters in Montgomery. They ran pictures of some Negro men sitting in the front of a bus. They looked tired, but pretty proud of themselves. Buses here in Little Rock have been integrated recently, but most colored folks I know still tend to sit near the back anyway.

I don't think Daddy could have done what Dr. King did—got a whole city to cooperate on anything. And would I have walked with them in protest? Maybe if Reggie walked with me. That's not the right reason, I know.

I'm not even sure Reggie is going to be in my life much longer, and the thought of losing him is making me crazy! He wants me to go to Mann with him. If I go to Central, I lose the friends I've been with since grade school, my chance to be a cheerleader for Reggie's team, and the only boyfriend I've ever had. Not much chance of me finding a boyfriend at Central.

MONDAY, FEBRUARY 4, 1957

Hey, Sylvia, what did you do your project on?" Calvin asked as they walked into the classroom. "I know you'll get an A-plus as usual, Miss Perfect Patterson." He took off his hat, bowed down in front of her, then dropped to one knee. "May I just touch your hand, my lady?"

"Oh, quit that," Sylvia said, laughing, as she swatted him on the side of his head. "Get up and go dust off my chair so I may sit down on a proper throne!"

Calvin scrambled up and ran ahead, pretending to strew flower petals in front of her. Sylvia tried to brush it off, but she didn't like being the center of attention, and she didn't like it when others made fun of her good grades. The thought of being chosen to be on the list to go to Central made her even more nervous.

Reggie walked in then, wearing his favorite shoes and that brown leather bomber jacket Sylvia liked so much. It had belonged to his father, he'd told her once, and Sylvia thought it smelled of adventure and history—maybe a little romance. She relaxed as he gave her a genuine smile and went to his seat.

Just then Candy Castle, whose soft yellow sweater clung to her cleavage like melted cheese, walked over to Reggie's desk and casually leaned over to speak to him. Her ample chest was level with his face. Sylvia couldn't hear what Candy said, but Reggie laughed as if she had told the best joke in the world.

Miss Washington, after taking attendance and making announcements, stopped at every student's seat to collect their projects, taking the time to speak to each student.

"You did your paper on baseball?" Sylvia heard Miss Washington ask Reggie.

"Yes, ma'am. Jackie Robinson. And the other Negroes who integrated major league baseball," Reggie replied.

"Good," Miss Washington said as she moved to Lou Ann Johnson's desk. "And what did you choose, Miss Johnson?"

The large woman standing so close made Lou Ann seem even skinnier.

"I did my paper on Fats Domino and Chuck Berry. They're going to change the world of music," Lou Ann replied. "Besides, all the rest of the stuff on your list was boring."

"Well, I certainly hope your paper isn't boring. I'd hate to fall asleep in the middle of reading it and be forced to give you a failing grade," Miss Washington replied, chuckling.

When she got to Sylvia's neatly handwritten report, Miss Washington asked with a tone of approval in her voice, "Why did you choose Africa, Sylvia Faye? Many Negroes want to forget their heritage and their roots."

"I read an article in the World Book encyclopedia and it made me angry," Sylvia replied. "I wanted to find something that would make me feel proud."

"Sadly, most people don't look at Africa with pride," Miss Washington said.

"I think it's important that we know where we came from, so we can figure out where we're going," Sylvia said simply. Calvin made an armpit noise. Candy Castle got out her hairbrush.

The teacher nodded with approval. "We need more sensible thinkers like you, Sylvia Faye," Miss Washington said. "That's one reason you were chosen to be a candidate for Central." As she moved around the classroom collecting the rest of the projects, Sylvia shifted uncomfortably in her seat. It seemed as if everyone in the class was watching her, making judgments with their eyes. Reggie, noticeably, looked in the other direction.

"Sylvia's always trying to be the teacher's pet!" Candy

Castle whispered harshly—loud enough for Sylvia to hear. In spite of Miss Washington's strictness, Candy was chewing a piece of gum. She worked it slowly, with her mouth half open. Reggie, and the rest of the boys who sat near her, could focus on little else. Sylvia glanced at her and rolled her eyes, but said nothing.

Miss Washington, however, had ears attuned to the smallest scrap of noise, and the proverbial teacher's eyes in the back of her head. Without turning around she said, "I'd suggest you concentrate on self-improvement instead of self-enhancement and the degradation of others, Miss Castle. And spit out that gum. You've got the whole room smelling of peppermint gum!"

Candy took the opportunity to walk languidly to the wastebasket in the front of the room. Her skirt, brown woolen plaid, hid no secrets. She sauntered as if she knew the world was watching. It usually was, Sylvia noted with a sigh. The chewed wad of gum, probably a whole pack, clunked loudly in the empty basket.

Miss Washington, who had seen it all before, tried to ignore her.

"I did my project on the Harlem Globetrotters!" Calvin said as he turned his attention away from Candy and back to the teacher. "Did you know they've been around since 1927? They are best basketball players in the world!"

"The world is a better place, I'm sure," Miss Washington said with a chuckle, "because of that team."

"Is she making fun of my report, Sylvia?" Calvin asked.

"As long as she gives you a good grade on it, don't worry," Sylvia told him, but she was focused on Reggie, who was passing a new pack of gum to Candy Castle, a big grin on his face.

Candy took the pack of gum with a smile, unwrapped a stick, then passed it back to Reggie, who gently placed it on her tongue. His eyes never left her face, her mouth, her lips.

Lou Ann leaned over to Sylvia and whispered, "You gonna let him do you like that, girl?"

Angry and embarrassed, Sylvia felt her face flush. "May I be excused to go to the restroom, please?" she asked the teacher.

Miss Washington nodded and Sylvia hurried out of the room. *I bet no boys are watching my every move as I walk past them,* she thought bitterly. *Not even Reggie.* When she got in the hall she let the tears fall.

Sylvia gave herself ten minutes in the bathroom, hiding behind the large wooden doors of the bathroom stall. Any longer and Miss Washington would come looking for her. When she walked back into the classroom, the teacher had begun a geography lesson, Candy was once again chewing gum, and Reggie looked up at Sylvia with innocent affection and a big grin, as if nothing had happened. She did her best to ignore him, but her heart was doing flip-flops.

"I warned you. Use him or lose him," Lou Ann whispered as Sylvia returned to her desk.

"I don't know how!" Sylvia whispered back helplessly.

"If you go to Central, Reggie's going to go for Miss Sweet Treat over there," Lou Ann replied. "You get chaos, Reggie gets Candy. Don't be dumb." Miss Washington peered over her glasses to stifle their whispering.

At lunch Sylvia sat with Lou Ann, punching holes in her peanut butter sandwich with a pencil.

"You through killin' that food, Sylvia Faye?" Lou Ann asked with a laugh.

"I have a lot on my mind," Sylvia admitted. She tossed the sandwich in the trash. "All this integration stuff is getting to me."

"Leave those prejudiced folks at Central alone," Lou Ann stated with a toss of her head. "How boring to go to school with white people!"

"They have a better school than we do," Sylvia countered.

"Bigger, maybe, but so what? I'm not complaining. Dunbar is good, but Mann is better! Look at all the fine boys we'll be able to pick from when we get there! I can't wait."

"I thought you already had a boyfriend," she said to Lou Ann, teasing.

"Oh, good old Otis is my junior high boyfriend, maybe even my summer vacation man. But he better watch out—Lou Ann is ready for high school boys now!" She threw back her head and laughed deeply.

"If I go to Central, there's nothing I can do to stop girls like Candy Castle from flashing that smile and flouncing her poodle skirts at Reggie," Sylvia admitted.

"You got that right," Lou Ann said with a knowing nod of the head. "If you choose to do this stupid integration thing, you may as well wrap Reggie up in a big red bow, put a three-cent stamp on his head, and deliver him to Candy Castle."

Sylvia looked up, alarm on her face. "You think?"

"I know," Lou Ann replied matter-of-factly. "Look what happened in class today. Is it worth it, Sylvia?"

"I don't know," Sylvia replied, confused as usual. "It seems like the right thing to do." Her voice trailed off.

"The right thing for who? For you? For your parents? For Negroes everywhere?" She snorted. "Who will remember, and who will care about the first kids to integrate Central High School? Nobody."

"I will remember," Sylvia said quietly.

"Why do you want to go to a school where you can't join in stuff? If you go to Mann, you can be a cheerleader, run the newspaper, go out for track, and still be head of the smart kids' club—whatever that is." She smiled. "You can go to dances with boys that look like chocolate ice cream instead of vanilla, with boys you can touch, boys who want to touch you back. You'd be giving up so much, Sylvia."

Sylvia nodded and her shoulders sagged. Just then Reggie walked into the cafeteria, laughing hilariously with a small group of boys and at the girl in the middle of the circle. It was Candy Castle.

"See what I mean?" Lou Ann said. "I wouldn't give up my boyfriend for white folks. I would stay and fight for my man." Sylvia slumped as she walked with Lou Ann to take their trays back. The bell rang for class, and Reggie left with the rest of the boys, never even noticing Sylvia.

MONDAY, FEBRUARY 4, 1957—EVENING

At supper that night, Sylvia, in a grumpy mood, managed to offend everyone at the table.

"Quit hoggin' all the biscuits," she snapped at her sister.

"What's the matter with you? I only had one," Donna Jean retorted. "Mama, can I have jelly on my bread?"

"No jelly on dinner biscuits—only at breakfast," her mother said without looking up.

"That's just dumb!" Sylvia said. She stomped over to the refrigerator, took out the grape jelly, and smeared it all over two of her biscuits. "The biscuits don't know what time of day it is!"

Donna Jean put down her fork. "Ooh, you're gonna get it!" she said to Sylvia.

"What's gotten into you, Sylvia?" her mother asked with concern.

"Nothing but jelly," Sylvia replied. "Just leave me alone!" Sylvia blinked hard to keep from crying. She didn't even *like* jelly on her bread. She glared at her mother and stuffed the biscuit into her mouth.

Her mother looked at her strangely, started to speak, but was interrupted by her father. "Don't talk to your mother in that tone, Sylvia Faye," he said sharply.

"Why is everybody picking on me?" Sylvia shouted with her mouth full. "Can't I just eat my dinner in peace?"

"It seems to me that you are the only person at the table who is disturbing the peace right now," her mother said quietly. "What's wrong, Sylvia?"

Gary, who had watched the whole scene with detached amusement, finally spoke up. "Mama, Daddy, give her a break. People at her school and folks around town as well have been pulling her in all directions. 'Be proud! Be black! Be white! Don't turn white on us! Stay with your own kind! Go to Central! Stay at Mann! Integrate! Segregate!' It's enough to drive anybody crazy." Gary smiled with surprising understanding at Sylvia, who had started to cry by now. Her shoulders heaved. "Besides, Mama, her boyfriend's got a sweet tooth!"

Sylvia looked up, her face streaked with tears. She swallowed hard, amazed that even Gary knew her problems.

"What boyfriend?" her father asked. "She's too young for such."

"It's nothing, Daddy," Sylvia said. "Boyfriends are stupid!" She wiped her eyes then said to her mother, "May I be excused? I'm not very hungry."

Her mother looked concerned, nodded, and Sylvia ran from the table and up the stairs to her room, her face wet with tears.

Sylvia lay on her bed for a while with the door open so she could hear the ordinary after-dinner sounds. The swish of the well-rounded bristles of her mother's broom on the linoleum floor. The click of the door closing as Gary, like he did every night, left for the evening. Her father's snores as he sat in his favorite chair. The theme music from the show called *The $64,000 Challenge*. She and Donna Jean watched it every week.

She knew Mama would come up and talk to her before she went to sleep, using all those comforting sayings mothers seem to know. She wondered how her mother had learned all the right words, and if she'd know what to say to her own children in such a messed-up world. Then, feeling sorry for herself, she started crying again, sure she'd never have kids anyway because she was too ugly and stupid to keep a boyfriend.

After Mrs. Patterson made Donna Jean turn off the television, Sylvia listened as DJ tiptoed up the stairs.

"You all right, Sylvia?" the younger girl asked as she entered the darkened room.

"Yeah. I'm sorry I yelled at you, DJ." Sylvia sat up and turned on the small lamp that stood between their twin beds.

"Please don't get like Gary, Sylvie. I couldn't stand it if you were mad all the time like he is." Donna Jean looked at the floor.

Sylvia, a little surprised, pulled her little sister next to her on the bed and hugged her. "I promise, Little Bit. And if you see me getting like that, you kick me in my shin, you hear?" She could feel Donna Jean relaxing.

"For real?" DJ said with a grin. "Can I practice?" She stood up and lifted her foot as if to kick.

"Not a chance, kid! Hey, how was our show this week? Anybody win the sixty-four thousand dollars?"

"You should have seen it! A boy named Leonard Ross, who was only eleven years old, won all that money!"

"That's so not fair!"

"Why not?" asked Donna Jean, who looked at her sister like she was crazy.

"I'm as smart as that kid, and older than he is—how come he gets the chance to win so much money?" Sylvia asked glumly.

"You ever see a colored contestant—ever?"

"That's my point. The world is all tilted and I don't know how to make it right."

"Well, maybe it's not your job to straighten it. You know, you never will see a Negro on one of those shows," Donna Jean said with certainty. She sounded much older than her eight years.

Sylvia smiled at her sister. "Nat King Cole has a TV show.

Does that count?" Their whole family always rushed to watch it, amazed at seeing colored people on the screen.

"Not for long. I heard Daddy say it was going to be canceled because no white company will sponsor the show, and no colored company can afford it. And you can't fix that, either, Sylvie," she added.

"You know, DJ, all I ever wanted was for people to like me, and maybe have a boyfriend who thought I was cuter than the other girls. I don't want to be a hero. I don't think I can change the world." Sylvia put her face in her pillow.

"So don't." DJ put her pajamas on. "Relax a little."

"Huh?"

"Take your name off the list. Go to school with Reggie and be a cheerleader. Have fun in high school instead of stress." DJ unbraided her hair and brushed it.

"But I can't," Sylvia said helplessly.

"Sure you can. It's your life. Live it for yourself."

"People are depending on me."

"You're the only one who has to live in your skin. It's up to you, not them." DJ climbed into her bed.

"How'd you get to be so smart?" Sylvia asked as she watched the younger girl pull her blankets to her chin.

"I watched you." DJ turned out the light.

Tuesday, February 5, 1957 Five A.M.
SCRAMBLED EGGS

Sometimes I feel like scrambled eggs
all runny in the pan

My life's the yolk
and I'm the joke
that's served with cheese or bran

Sometimes I feel like broken chips
all crunchy in the bag
My brain is fried
and raw inside
and forced to choke or gag

Sometimes I feel like pizza sauce
all thick with garlic spice
My mind is oil
that will not boil
and baked like rancid rice

Sometimes I feel like chunky soup
all green with lumpy peas
My thoughts are tossed
not worth the cost
and cooked for none to please

Reggie didn't call last night. The whole house is still asleep, except
for Mama, I guess, who never sleeps. She's probably downstairs getting
breakfast ready. But I like sleep and it's not like me to wake up this early.

Sometimes if I write a poem or a story, I feel better, but this one has
just shown me how confused I am. I don't think I'm the right person to
try to be an integrationist. I'm too ordinary, and way too confused.

Mama, just like I knew she would, came in last night and sat by my
bed after DJ had gone to sleep. She said very little—just rubbed my

back and hummed a lullaby that she used to sing when I was a really little girl. I don't remember her leaving, so I guess I fell asleep.

Donna Jean is the coolest eight-year-old I know. Little kids these days are so much deeper than my crowd was when we were that age. She thinks like a grown-up and she sticks to her opinions and beliefs. I'm not even sure what my opinions are, but I do know that nobody had better try to hurt her.

I wonder what's gonna happen with Reggie. I know I don't have the guts or the stuff to beat out a girl like Candy Castle. If that's what Reggie wants, then she can have him. But I want him to want *me*! I'm not very good at this boyfriend stuff.

I hear Mama coming up the steps. I guess I have to get up now. I don't want to go to school. I'd try to play sick, but I know Mama would see right through it.

SUNDAY, FEBRUARY 10, 1957

Hey, Sylvie, uh, can I talk to you?" Reggie whispered as Sunday school was dismissed and the young people headed upstairs for service. He wore a soft brown button-down shirt. "That is, if you're still talking to me," he said apologetically.

His face, which to Sylvia looked like a piece of soft milk chocolate, was hard to resist. But he hadn't called all week. She looked away. After all, it was his attraction to Candy that started the whole mess.

"I'm surprised you remember my name," Sylvia answered stiffly. She turned to face him. "I don't get it, Reggie. Sometimes you act like I'm fried chicken, and sometimes you treat me like I'm the grease in the bottom of the pot. Which one is it today?" Her voice, a mixture of confusion and sadness, was not what she wanted him to hear. She wanted to sound angry and tough like a lion, instead of sorry like a little kitten.

Reggie bowed his head, then looked up with that grin she couldn't resist. "I'm sorry, Sylvie. Really, I am. It's just I'm scared for you, for what might happen."

"You don't need to be frightened for me. I'm doing just fine being terrified all by myself!" she replied. Sylvia pulled her Sunday school book close to her and continued up the steps.

Reggie grabbed her arm gently and stopped her. Everyone else had gone upstairs. "Please, Sylvie. Don't be mad at me. You know you're the only girl I care about."

"Coulda fooled me!" But she stopped on the middle step.

"I like you so much I want to keep you close to me at Mann. I'll never see you!"

"I show up at church every Sunday." She tried to sound haughty and unconcerned.

"That's not the same. Your daddy looks at me here at church like I'm a bug that oughta be squashed with giant army boots." The image almost made her giggle.

"This isn't about church, and you know it!" Sylvia said, remembering the way he had ignored her all week.

He looked down at his shoes, then back up at her with a look of challenge. "You know, you're right. You want to know the bottom line? I don't want you hangin' around all those white people! Is that a crime?"

She wanted to smack him; she wanted to hug him. But she knew she couldn't let him tell her what to do. "White folks rule the world, Reggie. You better get used to hanging with them if you want to be somebody."

"See, that's where you and me see things different. I think it's stupid to pretend somebody like Rachel Zucker is really your friend. If you get to Central, she'll stick with the rest of the white folks—just like white on rice."

"What does Rachel have to do with this?" Sylvia asked, exasperated. "You don't even know her!"

"I've been in the store lots of times. I see her giggling with her little white friends who come in with their parents."

"So? She's allowed to have friends."

"Black folks have to stick together to stay strong," he replied, his face frowning and serious. "You don't need to do this. You need to stay at Mann with me and the rest of your own kind."

"I don't believe you're saying this! I thought I knew you—understood you!"

He glanced away from her. "Believe it, Sylvie. I want changes to happen around here—I just don't want you to be the one to make it happen."

"Why not me? And who made you the boss of me anyway?" Her eyes flashed with anger.

His voice softened. "Because I care about you, and I don't want them to hurt you. I'd rather hurt them first."

"What about Candy Castle?" Sylvia asked. Her stomach started to churn.

"You know I don't care anything about Candy," he said. "You're the only sweet thing I want."

"You could have fooled me." She forced herself to stay calm and not let him see the flip-flops her guts were doing.

He shifted his weight against the wall. "I guess I was a little mad at you," he admitted.

Sylvia looked shocked. "What did I ever do to you?"

"Nothing. Nothing at all." He paused. "It's just that I want you to stay here, and I think you're gonna go there, and it upset me that you aren't putting me first."

"You sure picked a funny way of showing your pain," Sylvia said sarcastically.

"I'm sorry, Sylvie. Can we start over?"

Just then Donna Jean came tearing down the steps, almost out of breath. "Church is about to start and Mama wants to know where you are!" she said breathlessly. "You better quit your lovey-dovey talk and get upstairs—pronto! They've already started singing!"

"Thanks, DJ," Sylvia whispered as she hurried up the stairs to the main auditorium. She turned to Reggie and said, "I need you to be there for me. I've gotta know you've got my back—no matter what happens."

"I want you to be my girl," he said earnestly. They had arrived at the door to the auditorium. Two ushers stood there, faces full of disapproval.

She brushed a speck off her skirt. "I'll think about it," Sylvia told him calmly. "Call me tonight." *I can't believe I handled this so well. Wait till I tell Lou Ann!*

Sylvia picked up a hymnal from the stack in the lobby and hurried to the second pew from the front to squeeze in next to her frowning mother. "I had to go to the bathroom," she whispered. Her mother looked unconvinced. DJ giggled.

The singing began then, and Sylvia settled into the pew feeling as if she had won a battle but not the war.

TUESDAY, FEBRUARY 12, 1957

Where are you going, Gary?" Mr. Patterson demanded. "Every evening after dinner you disappear, coming back at ungodly hours. What's your problem, boy?"

"It's not me that's got the problem," Gary replied sullenly, looking at the floor.

"What's that supposed to mean?" his father asked, leaning in close to Gary's face.

Sylvia, sitting on the plastic-covered sofa, watched the whole scene in silence. She hated it when they fought; it made her stomach hurt. Gary needed so much in a hurry, and her father was like their old car—slow and dependable.

Gary, bristling with impatience, yelled back, right into his father's face, "I've got to get out of this house! I can't breathe in here!"

"You seemed to be breathing just fine while you ate your mother's fried chicken!" his father retorted. "Show some respect, boy."

Gary sagged. "Look, Dad. You know I love you and Mama and the girls. But try to understand my side of it. There's a whole world of change happening out there, and I want to be part of it!"

"Believe it or not, I understand, son. I really do. I let Sylvia's name go on the list, didn't I?"

"That's nice for Sylvie, but what about me? What about my chance?"

"Be serious, son. They'd kill you over at Central—literally."

"Some stuff is worth dying for, Dad." Gary glanced over at Sylvia, then back at his father.

Sylvia gasped.

"Gary, you're like a fire truck driving down the street looking for disaster. The fire will find you soon enough. Don't ask for trouble."

"Trouble got here before I did," Gary replied darkly. He had sense enough to stop the argument there. "Look, Dad. I'm just going over to Anita's house. Me and Reggie and some of the other kids are going to hang out."

Reggie's hanging with Gary now? This is not good.

"And what will you do there that you can't do here?" his father asked stiffly.

"Breathe. Dream. Talk. Plan."

"Plan for what?"

"The future instead of the past, Dad. Me and my boys aren't afraid like you are." Gary put on his jacket. "Besides, Anita believes in me," he added pointedly. His father ignored the taunt but looked a little hurt, a little scared.

"I promise I won't look for trouble, but I won't run from it if it finds me. But I gotta go. I just have to."

Mr. Patterson sighed and opened the front door for his son. "Try not to be too late. Your mother worries."

Gary nodded and bounded out before his father could change his mind. Mr. Patterson sighed heavily, turned, then saw Sylvia sitting in the semidarkness.

"Gary's a good kid, Daddy," Sylvia began.

"I guess I'm getting old, Sylvia," her father said as he sat in the chair across from her. "I just don't understand young folks anymore." He rubbed his forehead.

"Did your father understand you?" she asked.

"He died before he had a chance to worry about how I'd turn out," Mr. Patterson admitted. "They killed him, you know. Hung him from the apple tree in front of our house."

"I know, Daddy," Sylvia whispered.

"Seeing him hang from that tree changed me forever." He paused. "But I couldn't afford the luxury of being angry and having an attitude. I had to help feed my family."

"You hardly ever talk about him," Sylvia whispered. "I was really surprised when you talked about him at church last month."

Her father nodded in understanding. "Gary looks just like my father did—thin build, almond eyes, freckles—and it scares me that he acts like my father, as well."

"Really?" Sylvia asked in surprise.

"My father got himself killed because he had a smart mouth and a cocky attitude. White people hated him because he walked with a swagger and wouldn't pretend to be less than a man."

"So that's why you're always on Gary?"

"I couldn't bear to lose my son the same way I lost my father," Mr. Patterson explained. He looked directly at Sylvia then. "And I'd curl up and die if something happened to you, Sylvie. I'm a man of peace, but I'd give my life to protect you! You know that, don't you?"

Sylvia couldn't believe her father was talking to her like this. *Mama must have put something in his Kool-Aid!*

Sylvia walked over and touched her father gently. "I love you, Daddy," she told him. He grabbed her hand briefly but firmly, then headed heavily up the stairs.

Sylvia sat for a few minutes longer in the darkened living room, aware of all the words that were not said, and she trembled. For herself. For her father and brother. For the whole family. The silence settled uncomfortably, like dust.

Wednesday, February 13, 1957

Searching for a Dream—A Poem for Gary

You grasp frantically
    to fight away the void of air
    and the collapse of earth
    and the sting of fire.
You reach wildly
    to grab the knife of anger
    and the sword of sorrow
    and the dagger of defeat.
You shiver silently
    to shield yourself from fear of failure
    and the guilt of family
    and the submission to need.
You pace nervously
    to run beyond the pain of memories
    and the death of dreams

and the loss of hope.
You search desperately
to find the answers to questions unasked
and the key to all possibilities
and the source of the invisible flames.

MONDAY, FEBRUARY 18, 1957

L ordy, Lordy! Would you look at that! The world is turnin'
and I'm livin' to see it!" Mrs. Patterson exclaimed as she
came into the house from work. She slammed a copy of the
current issue of *Time* magazine on the kitchen table and then,
very unlike the mother Sylvia was used to, she danced around
the table. The cover of the magazine was decorated with a full-
face picture of Martin Luther King, Jr.—in color.

Sylvia didn't know which was more surprising—Mama
showing off like that, or the fact that the very proper, very
white *Time* magazine had decided to put Dr. King on the cover!
Sylvia picked up the magazine and studied it closely. She
decided that Dr. King was a good-looking man, a little like the
man of her dreams.

"I wonder why they have him looking away from the camera, Mama," Sylvia wondered out loud.

Her mother looked at the photo closely. "He looks like
something in the distance is making him angry, and he fully
intends to make it right just as soon as the photographers are
done with him! Umph! I love a powerful man!"

Sylvia gazed at her mother in astonishment. "I've never
heard you talk like this, Mama."

Her mother flicked her hand as if to dismiss the thought. She was peering at the photo again. "You know, he didn't seem to be the least concerned with who was taking his picture, or even that he was about to make history by being on the cover of this magazine." She continued to marvel.

"I guess he had important things on his mind," Sylvia said.

The picture showed a man with a full face, strong cheekbones, and a large nose. He did not smile.

"I bet this man would really enjoy chomping down on a pork chop or a buttermilk biscuit," Mrs. Patterson said, smoothing the cover with her hands and smiling like she'd found a new recipe.

He wore a gray suit, a crisp white shirt that Sylvia figured his wife took great care in ironing, and a stunning red tie. Her father always wore a dumpy blue suit and a blue spotted tie. She loved her daddy, but Sylvia had never seen him look as bold and powerful as Martin Luther King did in this picture.

"Why is a bus in the picture, Mama?" Sylvia asked.

"I suppose because of his success with the boycott in Montgomery," her mother replied.

Sylvia pointed to the photo. "And look how they put a pulpit in the background, showing Dr. King preaching, which I guess is his other job when he isn't out changing the world."

"You know what, Sylvie?" her mother mused.

"What, Mama?"

"I think this is a picture that will make white people very uncomfortable." Mother and daughter exchanged glances of understanding.

Sylvia promised herself that the next day after school she

would take twenty cents of her lunch money and buy her own copy of the magazine. A man like that was worth it.

Tuesday, March 19, 1957

Maybe folks here in this country should just start over, like they are doing in Africa. In this week's *Life* magazine, I read about a new country that's just getting started—Ghana. I don't know much about Africa, but I learned so much when I did my report that now I'm trying to read books to learn more. Each of those little squares we see on the map of Africa is about the size of some of our states, but each one is a separate country, with different languages, ruling systems, money, and customs. Most Americans tend to think of Africa as one big mysterious country, but it's made up of dozens of individual fascinating places.

It's cool to think about the birth of a country. I wonder how they decide the rules and the rulers. It's probably a lot like the birth of a real baby. After the initial happiness, they get grumpy with morning sickness, like Mama was before Donna Jean was born. I wonder if Negro women who are about to have babies this year in Little Rock are worried about bringing another child into this world of confusion.

I noticed that Martin Luther King had been invited to the celebration for Ghana. There was a little tiny picture of him at the bottom of the page. The magazine referred to him as simply "an Alabama bus boycotter."

SATURDAY, MARCH 23, 1957

Sylvia was in a good mood. Reggie had called her earlier in the day and they had talked for about fifteen minutes—

about nothing, really, but everything he said made her laugh, even the alligator and crocodile stuff. He didn't argue this time about Central or integration or any of the racial issues that Gary seemed to be always angry about. Sylvia didn't like the fact that Reggie kept hanging out with Gary and the older boys, but she said nothing because she hated arguing with him. She was relieved that the Candy crisis seemed to be over.

The sun was out, making it look like spring might decide to show up after all. Sylvia had changed the sheets on her bed, and Donna Jean's as well, and everything in her room smelled fresh and clean. The radio blasted as loud as she dared, and she hummed along with the songs she knew. Donna Jean was spending the afternoon with the little girls from next door; Gary had disappeared to one of his political activist meetings, and her father had gone to the brickyard to put in a few hours.

Thinking of Reggie, she strolled down the stairs and into the kitchen loudly singing the end of her favorite song, ". . . that you'll always be there at the end of my prayer!"

"What kind of song is that about praying, Sylvie?" her mother asked. "It sounds more like a love song than a church song."

"Isn't it all right to pray about love, Mama?" Sylvia asked with a grin on her face.

Mama and Aunt Bessie were sipping tea and pasting green stamps into books. Both of them looked at Sylvia as if she had lost her mind.

"What do you know about love, child?" Aunt Bessie asked.

"It's just a song called 'My Prayer,' Aunt Bessie. It's by The Platters," Sylvia answered defensively. "All the kids at school think they're the most."

"The most what?" Mama asked with a laugh.

"You know, they dig them—they think they're really cool." Sylvia smiled to herself, knowing her mother and Bessie just didn't get it.

"You better not let your daddy hear you talk that foolish slang talk or sing those love songs. If it's not a hymn or spiritual, you know he'll call it a sin."

"Daddy thinks everything fun is a sin," Sylvia replied in exasperation.

"Probably is." Aunt Bessie chuckled as she sipped her tea. "You ought to hear some of the stories from the women in my shop as I do their hair. Oh, yeah. The most dangerous fun is big-time sin."

Sylvia's mother gave a warning look to her sister, then said to Sylvia, "You want to help?" She offered her a pile of green stamps. Mama brought them home from the grocery store and saved them to redeem them in books. When the books were full, they could be redeemed for gifts and prizes. "Glory streams from the table of daily life," her mother said cryptically.

Rarely did Sylvia completely understand what her mother meant when she quoted those sayings of hers. "Do I have to?" Sylvia asked with a sigh.

"No, but when I save enough books to get you a record player so you can play those ridiculous rock-and-roll songs you seem to like so much, you'll be sorry you didn't help."

Sylvia wanted a record player more than anything, so she

pulled up a chair and grabbed a pile of the stamps. She slid them across the wet cloth on the table to moisten them just enough so they'd stick in the book.

"How many books do we need to get a record player?" she asked, looking at the small pile of completed booklets.

"About twenty-five—the same number I need to get a new electric coffeepot." Her mother gave her a smile.

"No fair! You don't even drink coffee!" Sylvia told her, pointing to her teacup.

"Your daddy does."

"I think I deserve a record player more than Daddy needs a coffeepot. He likes the way you make his coffee on the stove, anyway."

"Hush while you're ahead, child," Aunt Bessie said then. "Paste and hope."

Sylvia sat down and ran a strip of stamps over the wet cloth. As she worked, her fingers quickly became tinged with green and slightly sticky.

"I heard they're going to try to integrate a few schools this fall in Virginia and Tennessee also," Sylvia's mother commented.

"I pray for those children. They should only have to worry about learning their times tables, not how to dodge rotten eggs or rocks being thrown at them," Aunt Bessie said bitterly. "You heard anything from the school folks here yet?"

"No, but I read in the newspaper that the Arkansas Senate passed not one, but four segregation bills. One made attendance not mandatory at all integrated schools," Sylvia's mother replied.

Sylvia looked up with amazement. "What? That means white kids can skip school and not get in trouble. No fair!"

"Who said anything about fair?" Aunt Bessie replied angrily, making her stamps so wet they refused to stick in the booklet. "They don't want us in their schools, and they're not going to make it easy for anybody who tries."

"What a cost. What a cost," Sylvia's mother said, shaking her head, "that we must pay for progress."

"Speaking of cost, did you hear they're paying the Jews over a thousand dollars each if they survived Auschwitz?" Aunt Bessie asked as she pasted another page of stamps, a little less wet this time.

Sylvia looked up with interest as she remembered that hot day in Mr. Zucker's store. She had learned in school about the horrors of the concentration camps during the war. Over six million Jews had been killed, similar to the millions of Africans that had been killed during the time of slavery. She wondered if that payment involved Mr. Zucker, and if it did, if he would apply for the money. It didn't seem like something he would want to remember or call attention to.

"They deserve more than that," Sylvia's mother replied with a shudder. "They were starved, tortured, and humiliated. So many of their families were gassed like animals, then burned in giant ovens. It's horrible what people can think up to hurt one another." She touched Sylvia gently with green-tinged fingertips.

Sylvia's mind reeled as she thought about kids her age being sold at auction, or being executed in a concentration camp, or being lynched like Emmet Till. And here she was, getting ready to volunteer to be persecuted for going to school. She shook her head.

"Not much has changed," Aunt Bessie said quietly.

Sylvia spent the rest of the afternoon with her mother and her aunt, pasting the stamps into the books, and soaking in the edges of their adult conversation.

WEDNESDAY, APRIL 17, 1957

Miss Ethel Washington held a sheet of paper in her hand, which trembled slightly. Sylvia could see only that the words on it were typed in two neat columns. The class was silent—even Calvin had no jokes today.

"May I have your attention, please," Miss Washington asked, even though the room was so quiet it echoed.

She spoke quietly and deliberately. "According to research done by the Little Rock Board of Education, five hundred and seventeen Negro students who live in the Central High district are technically eligible to attend Central High School." She paused. "Of that number, eighty students and their parents originally expressed an interest in being seriously considered. As of today, forty-two students are still willing to be considered to be the first students to attempt the integration of Central High." She stopped again, removed her glasses to wipe them clean with her handkerchief, and slowly replaced them on her nose.

"So will those students go to Central?" Calvin asked in a surprisingly quiet voice.

"Not so soon, Mr. Cobbs. There is a process that must be followed. The remaining students must be interviewed by a committee of the school board."

"Why?"

"To make sure that they are the right people for the job—because it will be difficult."

"Anybody in here on the list?" Calvin asked.

"The only student in our class who still remains on the list is Sylvia Faye Patterson," Miss Washington replied quietly. Sylvia sat up straighter at her desk as the rest of the class turned to look at her. She felt like a bug under a microscope.

Lou Ann glanced at Sylvia, then nodded her head in Reggie's direction. Sylvia turned to look. He was frowning.

Candy Castle leaned over and whispered to Reggie, loud enough for Sylvia to hear, "You know who to call when she's up at Central being Miss Chocolate Chip in the vanilla ice cream. You get lonely, I always got extra candy at my house." To his credit, Reggie tried to ignore her while some of the other boys chuckled at the less than subtle hints she was dropping.

Calvin said out loud, "I'm proud to know you, Sylvia. And if you ever need somebody to make you laugh, just call me and I'll tell you a dirty joke!"

Sylvia smiled at Calvin and thanked him.

Some students glanced at her with envy, others with pity. Finally she bowed her head—the stares were sharp and almost painful.

Calvin raised his hand again. "When are the interviews?" he asked. Sylvia was grateful that he was asking, because she wasn't sure if she could even talk at that point.

"Sylvia Faye must report tomorrow after school," the teacher replied.

Sylvia swallowed hard and glanced up at Miss Washington, who tried not to look concerned. But she noticed that her teacher's fingertips silently drummed her desk for the rest of the afternoon.

Sylvia gave her parents the information at dinner. She found she had very little appetite.

"What are you gonna say to them, Sylvie?" Donna Jean asked as she tried to cut her pork chop.

"I have no idea, DJ. I guess I'll try to convince them I'm a good person," Sylvia replied.

DJ finally gave up on her knife, picked up the pork chop with her hands, and bit into it with gusto. She ignored her mother's frown of disapproval. "You need to be more than good. I think they're looking for perfect!"

"White kids aren't perfect," Gary said sullenly. "Not even close."

"They don't have to be," Donna Jean told him. "They're white!"

"It is true that often we have to try twice as hard to receive half as much," their mother admitted. She scooped more gravy onto Gary's plate.

"I just want an equal chance," Sylvia said quietly. "Are you coming with me tomorrow, Daddy?" Her father had remained unusually quiet during the meal.

"Yes, child, I'll be there. I want that committee to know you've got a strong family behind you. I'll speak my mind if I have to."

"Really?" Sylvia was surprised.

"Have you ever known me to sidestep an opportunity to talk in front of a group?"

Sylvia shook her head. "No, Daddy." She couldn't believe he was being so supportive.

"Are you scared, Sylvie?" Gary asked.

"Terrified," she admitted. "I really don't know what to expect."

"You want me to go in your place?" he asked, only half-jokingly.

"I really do wish you could," she told him. She stirred her food, but ate very little.

"I'd tell those stupid white folks to keep their old school!" Donna Jean said suddenly.

"Donna Jean!" her mother cried out. "I won't have you talking like that! Mind your mouth, young lady."

"But, Mama," DJ wailed. "Why can't things just stay like they are? We're happy at school, and we don't have to worry about bad people hurting us. What's so great about being with white people anyway?"

No one seemed to have an answer. Gary started to speak, but was silenced by a look from his father.

"The world is changing, baby girl," Mr. Patterson said quietly. "Whether we want it to or not."

Mrs. Patterson motioned to Donna Jean to come to her. DJ climbed on her mother's lap and snuggled close. Her mother rocked her as if she were still a baby. Sylvia cleared the table. Gary went to his room, unusually silent.

After dinner her father retreated to his favorite chair to

read the Little Rock newspapers, but he seemed to have trouble concentrating. He flipped from page to page hurriedly instead of his usual careful, slow method of going through the paper.

Sylvia sat on the hassock near his chair and asked him shyly, "Daddy, do you think the kids at Central will like me?"

"Of course they will, Sylvia Faye," he told her, not looking up from the paper.

"That's not what I mean, Daddy. Do you think I'll fit in with them, with the things they talk about and like to do?"

Her father hardly ever looked right at her—he sometimes looked in her direction, but Sylvia always got the feeling that something else more important had his attention. But at that moment, he looked directly at her, then gave Sylvia one of his rare smiles. "If the kids at Central are as smart and talented as you are, Sylvia Faye Patterson, they'll be mighty special. And if they have any sense, they'll be proud to call you their friend."

Sylvia sat there stunned. Her father rarely gave her a direct compliment. She gave him a hug and hurried off to her room to check on Donna Jean.

Wednesday, April 17—evening
All I can think about is what it would be like to go to school with white kids, with kids who think Elvis Presley is cute and Frank Sinatra is dreamy. Kids who have blond hair and blue eyes. When they knock, the doors always open. They expect good stuff to happen for them, and it does—like a magic wand or something. These kids don't know what it feels like to have a store clerk make you put your money on the counter so they don't have to touch your hand. These kids don't ever think about

the fact that the history books we use in school have nothing about famous Negroes, and no pictures of colored people except for a few photos of slaves.

Maybe Reggie is right—I should just stay where I belong, where I'm safe and happy and accepted. I'd miss so much if I left the friends I've gone to school with since first grade. Parties. Dances. Clubs. Basketball and football games. I've heard the Negro kids would not be allowed to participate in any of this stuff at Central.

It's their school and their world. They have their customs just like we do—football teams and cheerleaders and dances and such. I guess I would feel funny if I was told that I would have to go to school with little green men from Mars. But I'm not green—I'm human just like they are.

I've never been inside Central High School, but besides the fact that it's huge, huge, huge—covering one whole city block, it's got to be just like any other school, right? Lockers. Shiny, waxed wooden floors. A library filled with thousands of books waiting for a thirsty kid like me to gulp them down. A cafeteria that always seems to smell like tomato soup, no matter what they're serving.

Teachers—some fair, some biased, probably a few who are angry—all smarter than me and maybe not willing, but able to teach me. And students. Not all of them would be horrible racists. Many will want to help, and would be kind? Right? Rachel, for example, will be there. She would stand up for me, wouldn't she? Would she be afraid to tell people that we were friends?

Last week someone painted another swastika on the door of Zucker's store, Rachel told me. This was the third time in the past few months. Rachel suspects the Crandalls next door—probably Johnny and his hateful hoodlum friends. She said the first time it happened, her father sat down on the ground and cried—that must be awful watching your daddy shed real tears. She and her parents stayed up all night washing the door and repainting it. Three times the door has been painted. Three times.

If Rachel can't be safe in Little Rock, how do I stand a chance?

THURSDAY, APRIL 18, 1957

Sylvia Faye Patterson!" the harsh female voice called out.

"Yes, ma'am," Sylvia replied, standing up quickly from the wooden chair at the far end of the long, empty hallway. Her mother squeezed her right hand, and her father squeezed her left, but she suddenly felt chillingly alone.

"Enter!" the woman commanded from the other end of the hall.

"Yes, ma'am," Sylvia said again as she hurried toward the voice. A large, curtainless window let in the full impact of the afternoon sunshine, so Sylvia could only see the silhouette of the woman with the strident voice. Her parents seemed to be miles behind her.

"Hurry, girl!"

Sylvia's patent-leather shoes clicked faster on the wooden floor. She reached down to smooth her skirt as she checked her hair with her other hand. She wore a new, neatly ironed, red-and-white candy-striped dress that her mother had made for her, white gloves because her mother had insisted, and her Sunday shoes, which pinched her toes, instead of her comfortable school saddle oxfords.

Sylvia reached the door, found the woman with the voice to

be thin, unsmiling, and wearing a pair of cat-eye glasses, and entered the interrogation room slowly. Dimly lit, the dull gray room seemed to be full of shadows. It felt more like a prison than an office. Sylvia took deep breaths, resisting the urge to turn around and run full speed back down that hall. She forced herself to smile pleasantly, refusing to let them see how scared she was.

Six examiners, five men and one woman, sat at a long wooden table. The woman with the harsh voice, Sylvia realized as her eyes adjusted to the dimness of the room, was Eileen Crandall. She glared at Sylvia with thinly veiled animosity.

One straight-back chair sat about five feet away from their table, alone in the center of the room. Sylvia was asked to sit there. Sylvia took off her gloves and waited.

"You are Sylvia Faye Patterson?" It was both a question and a statement.

"Yes, sir," she responded politely to the first man who asked the question.

"You go to Dunbar?"

"Yes, sir."

"Your grades seem to be quite acceptable."

"Thank you, sir." *I guess that's a compliment. Who can tell with these people?*

"Do you think you're better than white children?" he asked suddenly. Sylvia was stunned by the harshness of the question.

"No, sir. But I think I'm as smart as anyone else."

"Are you trying to be smart now?"

"No, sir. I just tried to answer your question."

"Don't try to get sassy with me, now." *This is not going well—I feel like I'm going to throw up.*

"No, sir," Sylvia started to hang her head, but she lifted it up and stared at them all, directly in their faces. *I don't think they like it when you face them fair and square.*

"Do you have a boyfriend?" Mrs. Crandall asked.

Should I bring Reggie into this? she mused. *Unless you count that football game, we've never been on a real date, never done much more than talk and laugh on the phone.*

She replied, "No, ma'am. Not really."

"Most girls your age are interested in boys. Who would you socialize with in an all-white school? You certainly couldn't date a white boy." Mrs. Crandall was nervously chewing the wood on her pencil. *Who would want to go out with a white boy? Good grief! I have trouble enough understanding the boys I know.*

"I wouldn't want to do that, ma'am," Sylvia replied to Mrs. Crandall, not really sure how to answer.

"Why not?"

"I don't want to date anyone right now," Sylvia said honestly. "I'm mostly interested in my studies."

"Suppose you saw a white boy you found to be attractive. Would you try to encourage a relationship?"

Sylvia thought of Mrs. Crandall's son Johnny and the pasty-faced white boys that beat up her brother. There was no way she could imagine wanting to date one of them. "No, ma'am." she replied emphatically. "I really just want to go to classes. My parents are very strict with me and do not allow me to court at all. That would not be a problem."

"How many times a day do you go to the bathroom?" another man asked.

Sylvia looked at him with surprise. "I don't know, sir. I've never counted." *Mama never lets us talk about bathroom stuff, especially in public. She says it's just not polite. These people are crazy!*

"We'd have to give y'all separate bathroom stalls if we let you use the toilets at all. Could you go all day without going to the bathroom?"

"I don't think so, sir," Sylvia replied. Then, although she knew she shouldn't have, she added, "Could you?"

The bald-headed man scowled in disapproval and scribbled furiously on the piece of paper in front of him, but he said nothing else.

"You understand you could not participate in any school activities?" the bald man asked.

"Yes, sir."

"No dances—we wouldn't want none of y'all touching our children."

"I understand." *Nobody wants to touch their precious children anyway!*

"No clubs."

"Yes, sir."

"No sports."

"Yes, sir."

"You can't be in any of the plays—they wouldn't have any parts for Nigras anyway!" He chuckled and seemed pleased with himself as he continued to take notes on the paper in front of him.

"The rules have been explained to me, sir," Sylvia replied.

Then she added, "But I think they are unfair." *They didn't like that one!* Sylvia grinned inwardly.

"Nobody asked you what you think," Mrs. Crandall said haughtily as she peered at Sylvia over her glasses.

"Do you have any white friends?" another man asked suddenly.

Sylvia thought of Callie Crandall, who was most certainly *not* her friend, then she thought with fondness of Rachel, with whom she felt comfortable and open. So Sylvia replied, "I've known Rachel Zucker most of my life."

"You mean the grocery man Zucker's daughter?"

"Yes, sir."

"She's Jewish. She doesn't count. Do you have any real white friends?"

Sylvia's mind reeled. *They don't count Jewish people in with the white population?* This was a bombshell to her. "Uh, no, sir. I guess I don't." *I wonder if Rachel and her family know how they are looked upon by the majority of the folks in town. Yeah, considering those swastikas on their door, they do.*

The thin, bald-headed man spoke next. "Why do you want to go to Central High School, Sylvia Faye?"

She relaxed a little. "Central High School is the best school in Little Rock, even in Arkansas. I want to go to college when I graduate, and become someone special or famous—someone who makes a difference in the world. I think that Central would best prepare me to do that."

"Horace Mann is newer than Central—it was just built last year. What's wrong with the schools that have been established for the coloreds?" It was Mrs. Crandall speaking again.

"I think education ought to be the same for all children,"

Sylvia said slowly. "I think there is a lot we can learn from each other."

"What can a white child learn from you?" Mrs. Crandall asked haughtily.

"Patience, maybe. And understanding."

All of them shuffled their papers then. Finally the fat man at the end of the table who had said nothing yet asked, "Is your brother Gary Patterson?"

Oh, no. Here it comes. "Yes, sir."

"He's got a reputation for being a troublemaker. That kind of stuff runs in families. Are you a troublemaker as well?"

How am I supposed to answer a question like this? Sylvia took a deep breath and answered. "My brother has never been in trouble with the police," she answered honestly. *At least not yet.* "And I have no intention of ever causing any trouble to anyone."

"Does your mother like teaching the colored children at Stephens Elementary?" the bald-headed man asked.

"Yes, sir. I'm sure she does. Very much." *I wonder what Mama's job has to do with this.*

"We hear she's pretty good at teaching, at least for a Negro."

"Thank you." Sylvia tensed.

"Do you think your mama is willing to risk that job?" the fat man on the end of the table asked.

"Risk it? How?" Sylvia looked confused.

"Some members of our community are opposed to integration," Mrs. Crandall replied with a nasty smile. "I have heard threats of job action against the parents of the children who try to integrate. Are you aware of that?"

"No, ma'am," was all Sylvia could say. She felt like an animal in the road, about to be smashed by a car. "Our family believes in faith and prayer." *I think I need a little of both,* Sylvia thought desperately.

"Yes, we're aware of your family's church connections," the bald man said then. "You know, your father also stands to lose his job at Dimming's Brickyard. We wouldn't do such a thing, of course, but we can't control all of the members of this community." Mrs. Crandall was smiling broadly. "And wouldn't it be just awful if something happened to that little church y'all go to?"

Would they? Could they? Yeah, I think it might be possible.

Sylvia was amazed at how much they knew about her family and was terrified of their power. She didn't know how to respond, so she said nothing. She refused to look down, however. She stared at each of them boldly, none of the fear she was feeling showing on her face.

"If you are chosen to go to Central, Sylvia Faye, there is no telling what might happen to you in that large school with so many hallways and staircases. You would have nobody to protect you." The bald man's voice was cold and threatening.

Sylvia waited several moments before answering. *I'm not gonna let these people get to me! She took a deep breath.* "I believe in the goodness of people, sir, and the power of young folks like us to overcome what grown-ups like you might not be able to."

The committee had no reply to that. Abruptly, the lead questioner said, "We have your application, Sylvia Faye. We will inform you when we have made our decision. Thank you for coming in."

Sylvia was dismissed like she was minor irritant. None of the members of the committee looked up at her, and none of them smiled. As Sylvia walked out the door, her parents stood expectantly at the end of the hall. She ran to them and let their hugs make her feel whole.

Friday, April 19, 1957

I still feel like I've been hollowed out like a Thanksgiving turkey and stuffed with sharp knives instead of soft dressing. When I got home from the interview, I couldn't eat, couldn't sleep, couldn't even sit still. I went outside after leaving my dinner untouched, and just started running. I wanted to run to Canada, to the moon, to someplace so far away that I could forget feeling like the dirt off someone's shoes. Mama stood on the porch and watched me run. She seemed to understand.

When I got back home, sweaty and breathless, Mama sat on the porch swing, waiting. I hugged her, then hurried upstairs to take a bath. I needed to get their breath off me, their dirty looks.

I don't understand why people are so mean to each other, why one group of people can hate another group of people so much. It makes my head hurt to think about it, but I see it everywhere now.

I can see it in the eyes of the bus driver who really doesn't want me on his bus, and the man at the Rexall drugstore, who thinks I'll probably steal something. I can feel it in the whispers of people who walk behind me on the street. I wish I was still young like Donna Jean, who is sitting in the middle of the living room floor, making long necklaces of Pop-it beads and only worrying about whether she'll run out of red ones.

I need to talk to Reggie, but he's gone off with Gary again. He's been spending way too much time with my brother. At first I thought it was cool they were close. But now I just worry. It seems like all I do is worry and stress over stuff. Why can't I just have fun like other kids?

Chuck Berry's new song, "Up in the Morning and Off to School," is a big hit with all my friends. Even Rachel likes it—last week at the store she was singing the words about the mean teacher and the after-school rock-and-roll party. I don't know what school Chuck Berry was talking about in that song, but Little Rock for sure has no places like that, at least not for colored kids. I don't think it's going to be much fun this school year for white kids, either—the situation is much too tense.

School's gonna be out in another month, but instead of a summer of listening to records with my friends, and giggling about boys, I have to worry about what looms in my future if I get accepted to go to Central High School. Me and Little Rock are gonna need lots more than rock and roll.

SATURDAY, MAY 4, 1957

We're leaving for the library now, Mama." Sylvia popped her head in the kitchen door. She hoped her mother wouldn't give them a long list of rules and instructions.

"You've got enough change for bus fare?" Her mother, with her arms deep in a pan of warm, sudsy dishwater, looked up and smiled.

"Yes, Mama."

"Don't waste your money on snacks and foolishness—I'm fixing a good dinner."

"We won't."

"And be mindful of your surroundings. Times are rough and not everybody is happy about what's happening in town. You hear me?"

"Yes, ma'am." Sylvia waited for the proverb that she knew was coming next.

"Malice lurks in the heart of the unbeliever, child. Be careful."

Sylvia grinned. "I promise, Mama. We'll only be gone for a couple of hours." Sylvia shifted from one foot to another.

"Hold Donna Jean's hand as you cross the street."

"I will, Mama. Can we go now?"

"Sure, Sylvia. I'm not holding you back. You're the one wasting your time chitchatting with me."

Sylvia groaned with exasperation, but managed to smile and wave good-bye. Donna Jean, waiting in the living room, covered her mouth to stifle the giggles. "Let's get out of here before she thinks of something else!"

The two girls raced down to the corner where a city bus, billowing smoke from its tailpipe, waited for them. They dropped their coins in the pay box and collapsed in laughter on a seat in the middle of the bus.

"I love going to the library," Donna Jean said.

"How come?"

Donna Jean shifted in her seat and looked out the window at the city rolling by. "It smells good," she said finally. "Like dust and ink and magic and stuff."

"I know what you mean. I like how a book feels when I turn the pages, and how the ink smells—almost like something good to eat."

"That's probably because Mama took us to the library before we could even walk."

"That's what happens when your mother is a teacher!"

"Ah, we suffer so!" DJ put her hands over her head and pretended to be a movie star. The two girls chattered and giggled the rest of the way to the downtown library.

When they got there, DJ headed for the children's department, while Sylvia browsed the stacks, breathing deeply of that almost intoxicating library smell. She was thumbing through a copy of *Caddie Woodlawn*—one of her favorite books when she was younger—when she heard a familiar voice whisper behind her, "Is your mother with you?" She whirled around, thrilled to see Reggie's face just inches from her own.

"No, I came here on the bus with Donna Jean. She's over in the kiddie book section."

"So I finally get you alone for a few minutes," he said, sounding pleased. Sylvia automatically reached up to brush her hair smooth, but he took her hand and said, "No, don't. You look great."

They had to whisper, of course, but to Sylvia, that made the whole event seem more exciting. She shivered with delight. "What are you doing here?"

"You told me you were going to be down here today, so here I am!"

"I'm really glad to see you," Sylvia told him. She didn't remove her hand from his.

"What's that book you're reading?" he asked. He leaned over to see it, and his shoulder touched hers. Sylvia could smell the Juicy Fruit gum he'd been chewing and the English

Leather cologne she had learned to love. The last time she had gone shopping with her mother, she had seen one of those sampler bottles of cologne and had sprayed a little bit of English Leather on her handkerchief. She kept it under her mattress and every once in a while she would pull it out and smell it.

"Just a girl book," Sylvia said softly. "She gets into all kinds of adventures." She was having trouble speaking. He was standing so close that it felt as if they were breathing together.

"Does she get kissed in that book?" he asked quietly.

"No," Sylvia whispered. She trembled.

"She should." Then, very softly, for just a moment, his lips touched hers. He smiled and said, "There's nobody but you for me, Sylvie. Nobody. You gotta believe me. Forgive me if I hurt you, okay?"

Sylvia felt a little dizzy. "Okay," she murmured.

He touched her lips with his once more. "I gotta go. I'm supposed to be at a meeting with Gary and some other guys."

Sylvia made a face because that spoiled the mood a little. But she managed to say as he waved and bounded out of the library, "Don't do anything stupid, Reggie." She had no idea why she blurted out those words instead of something romantic. *I'm so bad at this boyfriend stuff.*

"Was that Reggie Birmingham I saw leaving?" Donna Jean asked as she approached, holding a stack of children's books.

"Uh, yeah. It was." Sylvia could still feel the soft pressure of his lips. She didn't want to move her lips and make the feeling disappear.

"You've got that 'Little Richard Tutti Frutti look on your

face, big sis," Donna Jean said with a knowing smile. "We better head for home now."

"You're right," Sylvia said dreamily.

The girls took their time checking out their books and heading for the bus stop. They noticed a bus just pulling off as they got to the corner. "Looks like it will be another twenty minutes before another bus comes," Sylvia said, still remembering the feel of Reggie's mouth on hers.

"I'm already halfway finished with my first book," DJ said absentmindedly, leaning against the bus stop pole. "I'll be done before the bus even gets here. It's really good."

Neither Donna Jean, who was intently reading her book, nor Sylvia, whose thoughts were focused on Juicy Fruit and English Leather, noticed the three boys as they approached.

"What're you two little cotton pickers doin' on my street?" the first boy said. He had yellow, crooked teeth and dirty hair that lay flat on his head. Sylvia inhaled as she recognized Bubba Smith and his brother Sonny, who was taller but had the same bad teeth and hair. Next to him, Johnny Crandall, thick-shouldered and threatening, moved closer to the two girls. The three boys, large and imposing, surrounded Sylvia and Donna Jean.

"My brother asked y'all a question," Sonny said, knocking the books out of DJ's arms. She started to cry.

Sylvia put her arm around her sister, and tried to edge away, but the boys moved closer, trapping the girls. "Leave us alone," Sylvia said as loudly and boldly as she could. "We're just waiting for the bus."

"I don't see a bus," Sonny said. "Do you boys see a bus?"

"Not a bus in sight," Bubba said, menace in his voice. He put his face close to Sylvia's and laughed harshly. She could smell his unwashed teeth.

"What you think we ought to do with these two little black specks of dirt, fellas?"

Johnny reached out and stroked Donna Jean's hair. She jerked back in disgust.

"Don't you touch her!" Sylvia yelled, slamming her book against Johnny Crandall's chest and stepping as hard as she could on his foot.

He pulled his hand back from DJ and slapped Sylvia on the side of her head. "You tryin' to make me angry, girl? Don't you *ever* touch my blue suede shoes! I'll knock you to kingdom come!"

Sylvia felt as if her ear and face had exploded. She screamed out in anger and pain, "Get out of my way, you ignorant idiot! Leave us alone!" Johnny just laughed.

Bubba grabbed Sylvia's library books and tossed them to the ground with derision. "Don't you go getting' uppity now, girl!" he threatened. Sylvia wisely kept her mouth shut this time.

"Ain't you on that list to go to my school?" Johnny Crandall asked Sylvia. "I know your brother—he's a real troublemaker, and I bet you are, too." He leaned over and wiped off his shoe.

"That's none of your business!" Sylvia replied angrily. "Now move out of our way!"

But the boys didn't budge. If anything, they moved closer. "We don't want your kind at our school. You hear?" Johnny made the statement, and the other two boys made it clear they agreed.

Sylvia refused to let them see her cry, but she wasn't afraid to scream, so she yelled as loudly as she could, *"Help!"* And again, louder the second time, *"Help!"*

A blond, crew-cut-wearing teenager in a letter sweater from Central High walked out of the library just as Sylvia started yelling. He ran toward her. "What's wrong?" he asked with concern.

Johnny and his friends backed off then, but knocked both Sylvia and Donna Jean to the ground before they ran down the street, laughing.

The two girls, books strewn around them, dresses covered with dirt, sat there on the ground hugging each other. The boy from the library stooped down, gathered up the books, and helped Sylvia and DJ to their feet.

"Are you two all right?" he asked. He glanced down the street where the other boys had disappeared.

"Yes, we're fine," Sylvia said shakily. "Thanks so much. You got here just in time."

"Did they hurt you?" the boy asked.

Donna Jean brushed off her skirt. "They got my books all dirty," she said angrily.

"I've seen those three around. Nothing but trouble," the boy said as a car pulled up to the curb. "Hey, this is my mom coming to pick me up. Do you two need a ride someplace? We'll be glad to take you."

Sylvia could see their bus coming down the block. Breathing normally now, and feeling a little less shaky, she told him, "No, thanks, but I really appreciate the offer. Our bus is here now. Thanks again for rescuing us. Really."

The boy grinned as he got in his mother's car. "My name is Jim. See you around."

Sylvia and DJ climbed on the bus silently and shakily. Sylvia took out a clean handkerchief and wiped her face and her sister's.

"Are you okay?" Sylvia asked her sister finally.

"I'm scared," DJ said, wiping her nose. "But that boy was awfully nice."

"Yeah, he sure was."

"What woulda happened if he hadn't showed up?" DJ wondered.

"I hate to imagine." Sylvia shuddered. "Are you sure you're not hurt?"

"Not on the outside," Donna Jean admitted.

"I think we ought to keep this a secret," Sylvia said.

"And not tell Mama?" DJ asked in disbelief.

"What good would it do?" Sylvia retorted, a harshness in her voice. "It would just get her all upset." She glanced out the window every few minutes, checking for she knew not what.

Donna Jean sniffed and wiped her nose again. "I guess you're right, but it's awfully hard to hide things from Mama." The bus lumbered down the street and carried them home to relative safety. But both girls knew they would never feel completely safe again.

SATURDAY, MAY 4, 1957

Though still shaken by their afternoon ordeal, Sylvia and Donna Jean managed to help their mother prepare dinner, eat a full meal, and wash the dishes without letting anything slip.

"You're awfully quiet, girls," Mrs. Patterson did mention once during the evening. "Silence is golden, you know, but I miss it when my girls aren't giggly."

"I have a lot to think about, Mama," Sylvia said.

"You're right, dear. I don't want to put any more stress on you than necessary," her mother replied. "Keep your face to the sunshine and you cannot see the shadow," she said as she dusted the furniture.

"Yes, Mama," Sylvia said obediently, but she wondered what her mother would say about the shadow named Johnny Crandall.

Donna Jean grabbed one of her library books after dinner and curled up in a chair. "I just want to finish this chapter before bedtime." Sylvia noticed, however, that DJ only held the book and stared at the pages—she wasn't reading.

Reggie called a few minutes later, and Sylvia grabbed the phone and took it into the hall, glad her mother had gone upstairs. Sylvia's right ear still hurt, so she put the receiver on the left side of her face.

"How's my girl?" he asked, his voice soft like caramel.

Sylvia knew she had to tell somebody. "I wish you had stayed at the library a little longer," she began, talking softly so her mother couldn't hear.

"Oh, so you're telling me you want a repeat performance?" he said, chuckling.

"Well, yes, I mean, no, I mean, that's not what I'm talking about. Something happened after you left." She was close to tears.

"What's wrong, Sylvie? You seem upset." Reggie's voice now sounded worried and edgy.

She took a deep breath. "Me and DJ were waiting for the bus, and these three boys started messing with us and—"

"Who was it? The Smith Brothers?" Reggie's voice was tight on the other line.

"Yeah," Sylvia told him. "How did you know?"

"Not hard to figure out. Was Johnny Crandall with them?"

"Yeah, he was." Sylvia's ear throbbed.

"What did they do? Did they hurt you?"

"Mostly they just tried to scare us," Sylvia explained. "I tried not to let them know it, but it worked! They pushed us down in the dirt, tossed our books around, and threatened me."

"About the integration list?"

"Yeah."

"Did they touch you, Sylvia Faye?"

"Johnny Crandall slapped me, but I'm not cut or bleeding or anything."

"What about your sister?" Reggie was sounding increasingly upset.

"They didn't touch DJ, except to push her down, but she said she feels dirty. I know what she means. My sense of, I don't know, my sense that the world is an okay place, is all messed up. I was so scared."

"Nasty, hateful white boys!"

"Calm down, Reggie. Please."

"I wish I had been there. I would have kicked butt." Reggie was breathing hard.

"Actually, I'm glad you weren't there. There were three of them—they would have mopped the sidewalk with your body."

"I don't care. They might have beat me, but they would

have remembered the fight before I got finished. It drives me crazy that one of those low-life boys put his hands on you!"

"I'll be fine. I'm better now that I've told somebody."

"You didn't tell your parents?" Reggie asked incredulously. "Or Gary?"

"No. I was scared, and I know it wouldn't make a difference," Sylvia said helplessly. "And Gary is way too hotheaded. I'm not ready to bury him."

"Well, I'm glad you told me. I don't want you to *ever* go out alone, you hear? Little Rock just ain't safe, especially for you."

Sylvia sniffed back her tears. "I'll be careful. I promise." She was glad she had opened up to him. It felt right.

"And, Sylvie?"

"Yeah?"

"You better think long and hard about being one of the integrationist students. Maybe what I've been saying all along is not so stupid after all."

"I know," she replied quietly. "I've been thinking the same thing."

Saturday, May 4, 1957
I think I finally understand Gary's anger and hatred and his need to *do*! It's a good thing I like to write—it's my way of letting out all that stuff without screaming. I want to hit something, hurt something! I want to break a window or smash in some ugly, yellow teeth! I want to cry.

I can still smell their rotten breath, see the hatred in their little bitty eyes, feel their hands on us. And how dare Johnny touch my baby sister! She's too young to have to live like this. She's supposed to worry about stupid little-kid stuff like playing with her dolls and teacups, not about unwashed teenaged bigots knocking her around on the sidewalk. This is going to mess her up for a long time—maybe for the rest of her life. Memories like that don't go away.

I know I'm not going to forget. Ever.

Is this what it will be like every day at Central High? Walking down the halls with people who hate you just because your skin is darker than theirs? Maybe I'm not the hero Miss Lillie says I am. Maybe this is not the path I'm supposed to walk. So many folks are depending on me, putting me up on a pedestal I never asked to be on. It was never my idea to do this anyway—it was Gary who wanted to be in the front of the fight. I hate fighting. Does that make me a coward?

It could have been so much worse. If they had wanted to, they could have dragged us off and killed us. Nobody would have paid much attention to teenagers horsing around on a public street in broad daylight in downtown Little Rock. Not until it was too late.

Am I willing to die for all this? Honestly, I don't think so.

MONDAY, MAY 6, 1957

You got it! You got it!" Sylvia crowed excitedly.

Instead of the coffeepot, Sylvia's mother had redeemed the green stamp books for the record player. Made of pink plastic, it was sitting on the little table next to Sylvia's bed when she got home from school. She ran to her mother and hugged her tightly.

"Thanks, Mama."

"You've been under a lot of stress lately. You make good

grades, you help me around the house, and there's no telling what's going to happen this fall. Our yesterdays and tomorrows are written in the stars."

Sylvia ignored her mother's quote of the day and hugged her once more. "You're the best," Sylvia told her mother.

"Maybe the record player will help. But don't play that rock-and-roll stuff too loud when Daddy is home. You know he doesn't like it."

"I promise." She ran back to her room and even showed Donna Jean how to set a record carefully on the turntable, then place the needle on the record as it spun.

"You gonna buy a million new records now?" she asked as they listened to a Johnny Mathis song.

"No, not a million, but maybe a few. Records cost about forty-nine cents, so I'll have to save my milk money for a couple of weeks."

"Which one are you gonna buy first?"

Sylvia grinned. "'You Ain't Nothing but a Hound Dog,' by Elvis Presley! Daddy will love it!"

The two girls collapsed on the bed in laughter. Sylvia sat up when the telephone rang.

"You think it's Reggie?" DJ asked.

Sylvia didn't have a chance to answer out loud.

"Sylvia, come downstairs," her mother called from the bottom of the steps. "Gary, you and Donna Jean as well."

The children trooped down the steps and into the living room. Everyone's face was a question mark. "Who was on the phone?" Sylvia asked finally.

"That was Miss Ethel Washington." Their mother paused.

"The list of potential students to go to Central has been narrowed to seventeen. Sylvia Faye, you're on that list."

I Love Lucy was playing on the television, but no one in the living room noticed as Lucy tried to sneak once more into Ricky's band. No one laughed as she fell over with a huge headdress made of bananas. Everyone instead looked at Sylvia like she had won a prize or something. It made her feel uncomfortable.

"What happens now?" Donna Jean asked as she gave her sister a squeeze.

"Are you scared?" Gary asked Sylvia. "You want me to teach you how to fight?"

"Gary!" his mother said sternly.

Sylvia looked down at her small, brown hands and curled them into balls—fists obviously too weak to do any fighting. "I wouldn't know what to do," Sylvia said helplessly.

"She's going to need to know how to protect herself! I've seen what those people can do, and I'm not going to let them harm my sister!"

"All you're going to do is get her hurt," Mr. Patterson said sternly. "Why do you have to fight all the time? Isn't it possible that integration can happen peacefully?"

"No!" Gary yelled. "It is *not* possible!" Sylvia had never seen him so upset—and he was always angry at something.

"Shut up, boy!" his father demanded. Sylvia glanced at DJ, who blinked in surprise. Gary took one step back. Smoky feelings hovered over the quickly silenced room.

"I heard Miss Daisy Bates is going to try to teach the young people how to approach difficult situations with peace and nonviolence," Mrs. Patterson said, her voice purposely calm and quiet. "There is a meeting on Saturday at her home. I guess we'll find out more then. Peace is a powerful panacea."

"It won't work," Gary replied, his tone much quieter, but still argumentative. "And neither will your quotes, Mama. You're trying to fight battles with proverbs instead of swords."

Mrs. Patterson flashed her eyes at her son. "Don't push me, young man. You will respect me in my house, or I'll show you a side of me you don't want to meet!"

Gary bowed his head. "I'm sorry, Mama." Then he raised his eyes again, pleading with both his parents to understand. "You gotta try to see my point. This is no Sunday school picnic—it's a war for our survival! Even her boyfriend agrees with me."

Sylvia cringed, waiting for her father's reaction.

"What boyfriend?" her father asked, bristling even more.

"You started talking to me when I was fifteen, Lester," his wife reminded him. "But that's not the issue here. The problem is your boiling point, Gary. I worry about you."

"I'm sorry, Mama. But for once I'm right, and you and Daddy are wrong!" Angrily he opened the front door and stormed out of the house. The slamming of the door echoed throughout the house. *There sure has been a lot of door-slamming lately,* Sylvia thought sadly.

The perplexed parents looked at each other in helplessness. The world was starting to spin faster than anyone in the family knew how to handle.

Sylvia had barely said a word since the phone call. She honestly did not know what to say.

Tuesday, May 21, 1957

Gary is going to burst into flames. He wants to be in the middle of this fight so bad he can taste it. He wants to taunt white kids who dare to oppose his presence in their school. He wants to punch the first kid who calls him a name or who treats him like dirt. He scares me. I'm afraid he's going to do something stupid. And now Reggie is following Gary like a little puppy, copying the words and actions of Gary and his friends.

It seems to me you need to have a reason to be angry all the time. Until he started hanging with Gary, Reggie enjoyed life with his parents in a nice house, had plenty of spending money, and even an after-school job at one of the department stores downtown. The owner really likes him and says he'll let Reggie train for a management position. What's he so mad at?

Gary wants change right away. Maybe his way *is* better—it sure would be quicker. If people are going to hate us anyway, why not fight?

Sugar Ray Robinson, a Negro boxer, knocked out his white opponent last week in a championship prizefight. So now he's the world champ, and most of the colored men I know think Robinson is awesome. Even some white people admire him. So what's the difference? If they pay you to fight, it's acceptable, but if somebody like Gary fights, then it's wrong? Gary says he is willing to fight for rights and freedom and a better life. Robinson fights for money. Which is better?

I feel very alone. Lou Ann barely talks to me anymore. She told me I was "trying to be white," and I need to stay with my own kind. I try to talk to Rachel, but there's so much she just doesn't get about this situation. She gets to go to Central High in the fall. Nobody cares that she is Jewish. She got her class schedule in the mail last week.

I read in the *State Press* a couple of days ago that a black student at the University of Texas was removed from her role as the lead in the school opera because the segregationists said the part called for a white person. I wish my voice was good enough to sing opera. It seems to me that if she could sing well enough to get that part, she must have a pretty powerful voice. What does her skin color have to do with her singing voice? Doesn't singing come from inside the body?

The weather has been terrible—dark and overcast and rainy. In Missouri and Kansas yesterday, a huge tornado ripped through the two states and forty-eight people got killed. Dozens of houses and barns and businesses were destroyed. I listen to the news and read the paper and all I see is death and destruction and despair.

And I'm supposed to change the world? Hah.

Great Britain is testing nuclear bombs in the Pacific. I know that's a long way from England, but what about the people who live near where they are testing that bomb? I wonder if anybody asked them if they minded a big old dangerous bomb going off in their backyard. I bet they didn't. Maybe all this that's happening in the world is a sign that what we are doing here in Little Rock is not the right thing.

And I'm supposed to change the world? Hah.

Three of the seventeen students who were on the list have already removed their names. One girl quit because her mother's job was threatened. Another girl said she wanted to be a cheerleader more than she wanted to be a freedom fighter. I think she was just scared. And one of the boys quit because he said he had a chance to go to college on a basketball scholarship. He couldn't risk losing that one chance to make it. So far, it looks like I'm still going. It's terrifying.

And I'm supposed to change the world? Hah.

Sylvia awoke to an absolutely lovely morning—the last day at Dunbar for the ninth graders. The bad weather of the week before had disappeared. This was to be a day of finality and good-byes and uncertain futures for all of the graduates of Dunbar. The sun shone brightly, and if clouds awaited any of them, no one could tell by the bright possibilities of the sky that morning.

"Dipped in brown gravy and dressed in white." That's how her mother described Sylvia as she left for school that morning. She wore a white, flared spaghetti-strap dress with a crinoline slip. Her mother had worked for hours on her sewing machine, making sure it was perfect—and it was. Sylvia felt like a princess. She wished every day could be this delicious.

At school the girls strutted up and down the halls, all in lovely dresses of blues and greens and yellows—a rainbow of giggles and press-curled hair. They flirted with the boys, who wore slippery-soled new shoes, and spent lots of time in the bathroom mirrors, applying the pale pink lipstick and pancake makeup that Lou Ann had brought in her purse.

All the boys wore dark suits, white shirts, and skinny little ties. Calvin was so proud of his new suit he kept the price tag on it—$9.98 from Sears! Sylvia knew she would miss silly old Calvin. *If I go to Central, who will make me laugh?* she thought desperately.

Candy Castle showed up, the last one to arrive at the building, of course, in a cherry-colored velvet party dress. She made no pretense of hiding the lipstick and bright red fingernail polish she wore. "What difference does it make if I'm late?" she said with a laugh. "It's the last day of school." Sylvia chuckled to herself, figuring if she was a princess today, then Candy had to be the Wicked Witch of the West. Candy cheerfully ignored the looks the girls gave her, and passed out pieces of red-and-white peppermint candy to anyone who wanted them—mostly the boys.

Sylvia jumped when she realized Reggie had eased up close behind her. "You look lovely in white," he whispered. "She looks like a clown."

Sylvia relaxed, turned to face him, and smiled. "Actually, I feel a little sorry for Candy," she said.

"How come?"

"Well, she lives with an elderly aunt and uncle who basically ignore her. I think she just needs someone to love her—as long as it's not you," Sylvia added shyly.

"No worry about that," Reggie replied. "I'm working on somebody else right now!" He grinned.

"And who would that be?"

"Miss Ethel Washington!" he cried out. Then he ran down the hall laughing. Sylvia watched him run, enjoying every step he took.

"Looks like you got Reggie's nose sewn up tight—for now," Lou Ann said as she approached.

"I'm working on my stitches!" Sylvia replied with a grin. She was glad Lou Ann was in a good mood and speaking to her today. "You've been a big help, Lou Ann."

"I guess you're on your own now, kid," Lou Ann said, frowning a little. She wandered off to get autographs.

Each graduate had an autograph book and they spent most of the day getting signatures from every single person they knew—teachers and students both. Some kids just signed their name on the colorful pages, but some tried to be clever and write little verses. Calvin Cobbs wrote in Sylvia's book, "I like you, I like you, I like you so well; If I had a peanut, I'd give you the shell." She knew she would really miss sweet, silly Calvin.

Lou Ann wrote, "Sylvia, Sylvia, sitting on a fence; trying to go to high school without any sense." Then she taped two pennies under her name—for luck—and said, "One is for school sense, the other is for boy sense. You might want to use both of them for boys because school doesn't look like it will be much fun for you."

Sylvia sighed because Lou Ann always spoke the truth. She'd saved a whole page for Reggie—a green one. He took almost fifteen minutes to write the message, then he folded the page into a triangle. When he gave the autograph book back to her, he looked a little embarrassed. "Don't show this to all your friends, okay?"

"I promise," Sylvia assured him.

She opened it a few minutes later. She thought the message would be long and complicated, but all it said was, "I dream of a future with you." He'd signed it, "Love, Reggie—1957." Sylvia's heart thundered with delight and she held the autograph book close to her body. She had never read anything so sweet and wonderful. And he'd used the word *love*.

Miss Washington, according to tradition, took each student aside to say "one nice thing" before graduation. It was very private and students took Miss Washington's words quite seriously. But Calvin, who just couldn't keep his mouth shut, told Sylvia what she said to him: "Calvin, never lose your gift of laughter and love of flowers. They will save you from despair." Sylvia thought that was a little depressing, but she didn't tell him.

When Sylvia walked in to ask Miss Washington to sign her autograph book, she was a little nervous. First, Miss Washington told Sylvia that her dress was lovely, complimenting her mother on her fine sewing skills. Sylvia blushed and thanked her, but she figured that was a compliment to her mother, not for herself.

Then Miss Washington looked at Sylvia and said, "Sylvia Faye, I know you dream of greatness. Many students do. But you are one of the few that will succeed. I am proud to know you."

Sylvia was stunned. She thanked the teacher and hurried out of the room. Unlike Calvin, she didn't tell anyone what Miss Washington had said.

At the end of the day an awards ceremony was held. Her parents and Donna Jean all came—even Gary showed up, scowling whenever one of his former teachers wanted to give him a hug. The boys in their class received certificates for excellence in categories like carpentry and agriculture, as well as honors for math and science and spelling. Reggie, the best in the class in science and math, received a special honor award trimmed in gold. His mother, beaming with pride, took lots of pictures with her Brownie camera.

Sylvia received certificates for typing and sewing, as well as excellence in English, history, spelling, and a special award for poetry. What seemed to make her parents most proud was when they called her name for the National Junior Honor Society. Sylvia walked to the front, her white dress swaying gently from the huge petticoat she wore, and proudly accepted the honor. Her mother cried.

Thursday, June 6, 1957

I write poems all the time, but I feel like most of them aren't very good. I don't really know because I haven't got nerve enough to show them to my teachers, and I know I'll never show anything about love or kissing to my mother. She just wouldn't understand. I'll never be able to put verses together like Langston Hughes or write prose like Zora Neale Hurston, but somehow, Reggie makes me feel poetic. I wrote these after our graduation from Dunbar. Little Rock isn't even close to an ocean. I must be crazy!

Reggie

Puppy dog grin
Cheerful and thin
Golden bright coins
In his heart.

Arms strong and tall
In case I should fall
A warm pleasant glow
From the start.

We'll walk by the sea
Just him and just me

With sandspray
Erasing our steps.

He'll tell me his fears
And soften my tears
As the moon smiles
On promises kept.

So young we are now
But a friendship is how
A treasure grows
Wrapped with gold lace.

HE MAKES ME TREMBLE

He makes me tremble.
His breath, soft upon my lips
His arms, bold around my waist
His smile, warm upon my face.
His kiss, moist upon my mouth.
His touch, hot within my heart.
    He makes me tremble.

MONDAY, AUGUST 5, 1957—AFTERNOON

Wasn't that the best television show you ever watched in your life?" Donna Jean screamed with delight. "Maybe I *am* learning how to be a teenager like you!" She seemed to be pleased with that idea.

"And if Reggie hadn't called me to tell us about it, we woulda missed it," Sylvia reminded DJ. *"American Bandstand—* what a cool show! A dance show for teenagers. I tell ya—this modern world is amazing." Sighing with satisfaction, Sylvia flopped on her mother's sofa.

"Daddy's gonna say it's leading to sin and destruction for sure," DJ said.

"Daddy thinks everything that's cool is gonna send you to the devil."

DJ laughed. "It will be coming on every day after school, and Daddy doesn't usually get home until later, so we're set for a while."

Sylvia hummed a little of the song that had been featured, "I'm Gonna Sit Right Down and Write Myself a Letter." Then she sat up and said to her sister, "I guess you noticed there were no colored teenagers on the show."

"Of course not. The world is not *that* modern," DJ said, a tone of resignation in her voice.

"But almost half of the Top Ten songs were by colored singers," Sylvia reasoned. "The Coasters, Nat King Cole, LaVern Baker—if white kids can dance to the music of the Negro singers, why can't colored kids dance as well?"

"Now you're sounding like Gary," DJ said. She got up and clicked off the television. "Can you believe summer vacation is almost over?" Donna Jean asked.

"I have a feeling this school year is gonna be really different from any other we've ever known," Sylvia replied thoughtfully.

"For you, maybe. But I still get to go to school with my friends."

"I'll make new friends," Sylvia said, but without much confidence in her voice.

"Fat chance! You'll be lucky if Rachel has time for you. With your luck, you'll end up with Johnny Crandall sitting next to you in every class!"

"I sure hope not. Don't be so negative, DJ." Sylvia picked at the plastic on the sofa.

"I'm sorry, Sylvia." DJ flopped down on the plastic. "You know, it's still not too late to change your mind. How many kids are still on that list?"

"Twelve or thirteen, last I checked. The group keeps getting smaller and smaller. But the ones on the list are such cool people. It makes me feel good just to hang with them."

"You got another meeting at Miss Daisy Bates's house?"

"Tomorrow, I think."

"What do you talk about when you're there?"

"Nonviolent techniques. How to accept negativity with a positive spirit. How not to fight back. Stuff like that. And we eat. Miss Daisy makes great brownies."

"Gary would have lasted maybe ten seconds in a group like that," DJ said with a laugh.

"He knows that—even admits it. Where is he, anyway?" Sylvia asked.

"Either with his girlfriend—they seemed to be joined at the hip—or at one of those protest meetings again. I have a feeling they *don't* talk about smiling when somebody calls you a name. I heard Gary whispering something about explosives when he was on the phone last night," DJ said, her tone serious.

"Really? Maybe we should tell Daddy and Mama."

"I doubt if it would make a difference," Donna Jean replied, her voice sounding way too adult for her eight years, Sylvia thought sadly.

"He's going to end up in jail," Sylvia said fearfully. "He can see nobody's viewpoint except his own."

"That's the problem with everybody in Little Rock," DJ said. "Everybody's right. Everybody's angry. Everybody's scared. I'm moving to Alaska!" She got up and stretched.

Sylvia laughed. "Too cold for me. But you're right. White folks are scared of us. Today in the newspaper some guy ran a huge ad, trying to stir up trouble."

"You mean more mess than we already got?"

"Listen to this." Sylvia picked the newspaper up from the coffee table and read the ad to her sister. "'At social functions would black males and white females dance together, would black students join clubs and travel with whites, would black and white students use the same restrooms, would black males and white females enact 'tender love scenes' in school dramas?'"

"Give me a break!" DJ said, rolling her eyes.

Life seemed so simple on television, Sylvia thought. *But in real life, in Little Rock, folks seemed to be acting like they were about to go to school with Martians.*

FRIDAY, AUGUST 16, 1957

It had been hot and rainy in Little Rock for several days, and everything seemed to be covered with thick, red Arkansas mud. But Sylvia didn't let the rain upset her, because she had bought Nat King Cole's new album, and had spent the day listening to "When I Fall in Love" and "Love Is the Thing." She played it so many times that her mother finally peeked her head in Sylvia's room.

"What's got you in such a romantic mood?" she asked with a smile.

"Nothing," Sylvia told her. "I just love this album."

"You sure it's the album you're in love with?" her mother asked, her voice teasing.

Sylvia grinned. "I'm in love with the whole world today!"

"It's a wonderful feeling, isn't it?"

"Yes, Mama. It is."

Sylvia thought for a moment she would say more, tell her more about what she was feeling, let her ask the questions she'd been afraid to ask, but her mother just said, "Be careful, Sylvia Faye. True love is friendship set on fire."

Sylvia had long ago given up trying to decipher those quotes. So she just nodded and said, "I understand, Mama. You don't have to worry about me."

"Can you run down to Zucker's store for me, Sylvie?" her mother asked then. "I need some flour, some sugar, and a big bottle of vanilla extract. I guess a couple of lemons and a dozen eggs as well. I'm going to make a couple of cakes tomorrow for the bake sale at church, and one for Sunday dinner. Get an extra large bag of sugar. I know how you like my cakes super sweet."

"Sure, Mama," Sylvia replied. She hadn't seen Rachel in a couple of weeks. "You need something from Miss Lillie's, too?"

"No, just give her my best."

Her mother gave her a few dollars, then said with great seriousness, "Hurry now, Sylvia. Zucker's closes early on Friday, and I want you back well before dark."

"It's just a couple of blocks away, Mama," Sylvia said as she grabbed a sweater and tossed it over the shoulders of her favorite yellow dress. But she had to admit—she was a little scared.

Donna Jean looked concerned. "Are you sure it's safe, Sylvie?" she whispered as Sylvia got ready. "You remember what happened that day at the library?"

"I'll be fine, DJ," Sylvia told her as she headed for the door.

"I promise I'll be careful." Sylvia gave her sister a hug. "If I have an extra ten cents left over, I'll get you the latest Archie and Jughead comic book, okay?"

Donna Jean nodded, but frowned. Sylvia headed out in the dim late afternoon sunlight that had managed to peek through the leftover rain clouds.

As she got to the corner of the next block, Sylvia paused and inhaled with fear. Cruising slowly down the street, rock-and-roll music blasting loudly from the radio, was Johnny Crandall's black '56 Ford. *It's a free country,* Sylvia thought. *Well, it is for white boys like Johnny.* She started to go back home, then she got angry. Almost at the store, she pulled her sweater closer to her body and trod purposefully down the sidewalk. She figured if she ignored him, he'd get bored and go away.

But Johnny didn't want to be ignored. "Hey, little girl in yellow. Where you goin'?"

Sylvia walked faster and said nothing. She thought of Lavern Baker's new song, "Jim Dandy to the Rescue." No such luck for her—no hope that boy named Jim would swoop in and save her this time. "I'm talkin' to you, girl. You want a ride?" He drove very close to the curb, his car windows open. He had turned the music down.

"Go away," she cried out. She was one block from the store—a five-minute walk.

"You owe me a new pair of shoes, girl. You messed up my shoes. You think I forgot because it was a couple of months ago, but I ain't never gonna forget that." His voice was taunting, threatening. "And you better not show up at my school!"

"Leave me alone. Please." Sylvia's heart thudded.

He laughed harshly. "I'm warning you, girl. I'm gonna catch up with you one day when you least expect it, and I'm going to beat you like I did your brother. Your ugly little sister, too. It's just a matter of time." He sped off then with a screech of tires. She heard the music blasting once more as the car turned the corner.

Tears burned in Sylvia's eyes as she reached Mr. Zucker's store. Johnny had parked his car in front of his father's barbershop by that time. The radio was silent, the motor was off, and Johnny was nowhere to be seen. Sylvia felt a little safer, knowing she was surrounded by friends like the Zuckers and Miss Lillie—people who would protect her—but she still planned to call home and ask her mother to come pick her up.

She waved quickly at Miss Lillie, who was working on a new display in her window, and hurried inside the Zuckers' store. Rachel met her at the newly painted front door, grabbed Sylvia's hand, and squeezed it warmly. Sitting by the cash register was a fresh bouquet of roses—pink this time.

"You're shaking, Sylvia. What's wrong?" Rachel asked with concern.

"Nothing, really. I just had a run-in with Johnny Crandall. He scares me."

"I know how you feel. Papa is sure that he and his juvenile delinquent friends have something to do with the Nazi signs on our door, but there's no way to prove it. I just try to stay out of his way."

"He makes me feel dirty—like I need to take a bath after I talk to him. And I want to use your phone if I could before I leave. I don't want to walk home by myself."

"Good idea. Now, let's not spoil our conversation with talk of disgusting boys like Johnny. How's your family?"

Sylvia relaxed a little. "Gary's as hardheaded as ever, Donna Jean has discovered Archie comics, and parents don't change, do they?"

"Mine sure don't. How's Reggie?" Rachel asked.

Sylvia sighed. "He's hard to figure out. Sometimes he's like a cuddly little teddy bear, and I just want to squeeze him. But other times he's like an ugly old spiny toad, acting more like Gary and ready to fight all the time. That worries me."

"Maybe he's not good enough for you, Sylvie," Rachel said. "Maybe he's just practice for the right one."

"Hmm. I never thought about it that way. A practice boyfriend—like training wheels on your bike!" Sylvia made a funny face. "But I really have no complaints—he's never been sweeter to me. He's even kissed me a couple of times," she announced triumphantly.

"Did you see fireworks, like the actresses do in the movies?" Rachel asked with a giggle.

"It happened so fast I never even noticed!" Both girls laughed heartily and chattered as they walked slowly down the store aisles looking for the items Sylvia's mother had requested. *It felt good to be there with Rachel,* Sylvia thought, *relaxing a bit.*

"Did you see *American Bandstand* yesterday?" Rachel asked.

"I never miss it! Even Donna Jean watches it like a teeny teenager. She knows the names of all the regular dancers and is learning the words to every single song on the hit parade!"

Rachel laughed. "My favorite song, at least this week, is 'Whispering Bells' by the Del Vikings. I'm waiting to be kissed like you so I can hear those bells, too!"

"Did you know that group has both colored and white singers?" Sylvia asked. "Nobody seems to have a problem with it, and they're really popular."

"Yeah, I have their album. They make it look, and sound, so easy to mix it up like that." She started to say something else, but her mother headed toward them. "Here comes Mother with a plate of cookies and one of those suffocating hugs!"

Sylvia endured the hug, thanked Mrs. Zucker for the cookies, then turned to her friend. "You excited about high school?" she asked as she nibbled on a butter cookie.

"Oh, yeah. I am *so* ready! You're way ahead of me in the boyfriend department." Both girls avoided the obvious subject at hand for the moment.

Sylvia and Rachel walked leisurely around the store, picking up a couple of lemons, and searching in vain for the vanilla extract.

"Between my alphabetical filing system and Daddy's madman method of stocking the shelves," Rachel said with a smile, "nothing is ever in the right place."

They found the eggs and flour, a friendly silence sitting comfortably between the two girls. They walked back leisurely toward the front of the store with Sylvia's purchases in their arms.

I have to ask her this! What are we friends for if I can't ask her the hard questions? Sylvia stopped, put her hand on Rachel's arm, and asked finally, "Rachel, what do most of the your friends—the white kids—say about all this integration stuff? I mean, I know how Johnny and his bunch think. And I ran into a white boy a couple of months ago who didn't seem to care if I was purple or green. He went out of his way to be nice to me. So what's the real deal?"

Rachel looked directly at Sylvia. "Believe it or not, most of the kids I know don't care one way or the other whether the school is integrated or not."

"For real?" This wasn't the answer Sylvia expected.

"What I mean is, it's like that singing group. Nobody really makes a big deal of the fact they're a mixed-race group."

"I see your point. But this is Little Rock, not some big city like Philadelphia or New York."

"True, but most of the kids from my school that are going to Central really don't want to get involved with political problems. They're teenagers—they care about dates to the school dance and whether they have pimples—at least that's what I get from the kids I talk to. I think most of the opposition is coming from a small number of loud, hateful folks who can't stand blacks or Jews, either, like the Crandall family."

Sylvia was about to tell her exactly what she thought of the Crandalls when the world went crazy. She heard a crash, followed immediately by the crackling and breaking of glass, and then a thud, like the sound of a bowling ball being dropped. It all happened faster than she could process.

The explosions that surrounded her the next moment caused her to drop the eggs in her hand as she was tossed to the floor. Her head connected with the floorboards before the rest of her body. A shelf full of groceries fell over onto Sylvia.

As if she were outside of herself watching the horrible scene, she knew she was screaming, knew she was falling.

The noise of the toppling shelves and dry goods frightened her more than the feeling of crumpled wood on her legs. Most of it fell around her rather than upon her. Even so, sheer terror overwhelmed her. Her screams became clogged as debris filled her mouth, and she was finding it hard to breathe.

Stunned for a moment, Sylvia at first could see nothing. Gradually she dimly became aware of eggshells and gooey egg yolk in her hair and on her clothes. Something wet and drippy snaked down her back. Her mouth was full of a thick and powdery substance. She couldn't move her legs. Her head throbbed. Rachel seemed to have disappeared.

Sylvia's thoughts were as jumbled as the broken bits of the store that lay around her. Could an earthquake have hit Little Rock? Maybe it was a bomb? *Are we at war?* All she knew for sure was that she was afraid it was blood that was dripping from her body, and she yearned for her mother, who would know what to do.

Sylvia heard footsteps. She twisted her body toward the sound, tried to open her mouth to speak, but all she could do was cough a little. She saw a broken bag of white powder next to her face and figured it must be flour, not dirt in her mouth. But that didn't make it any easier. No words, no sounds, escaped her lips.

A second thud make the floor tremble, and the explosion that followed was louder than the first. Sylvia put her hands over her head and ears and trembled in the pepper and paprika. She had always wondered how she would feel at the moment of her death. Now she knew. She could hear more shelves collapsing, more pieces of the world falling in on itself. The floor smelled of fresh floor wax.

When the noise and movement stopped, Sylvia found her legs were covered with broken bottles and boards. She kicked at them angrily. She knew that Rachel's parents had to be searching frantically for them. As Sylvia managed to twist herself to the side, she had a clear view of the rubble-covered floor from the front of the store to the back. She saw two sets of feet fleeing from the store. Neither pair belonged to Rachel's parents.

Near the front door was a pair of highly polished, chestnut-brown, double-laced oxford shoes. Sylvia inhaled sharply. The shoes crunched over broken glass and spilled powders, then rushed outside. Sylvia could still hear the sound of the taps on those shoes, however, as they clicked on the wooden floor. Running to the back door was a pair of dirty blue tennis shoes.

A spilled box of pepper by her nose made Sylvia sneeze. The small room was filling with smoke. She knew she had to get out of there immediately. Sylvia twisted her body once more and found she could wriggle out from under the shelf. She pulled her legs free of the wood, relieved to see that her knees still bent and her ankles still flexed normally. As she slid her body out, she was glad she hadn't been standing next to a shelf full of large cans of candied yams or green beans.

Sylvia sat up carefully and tried to catch her breath, but she coughed once more as a sharp, acrid odor filled the small room. The smell reminded her of the barbecues her father prepared on holidays—how her mother always fussed at him because he used too much kerosene to start the fire. Fire. It was then the odor of burning wood and oil assaulted her. *Oh, my God! The store's on fire!*

Scrambling to her feet, Sylvia looked around frantically. Dark smoke, like a greedy ghost, gobbled the air. Eyes stinging, Sylvia could see flames two aisles over, eagerly destroying the dry goods on the shelves. Sylvia looked behind her and there lay Rachel, a jagged cut on her forehead. Her eyes were open, but she didn't move.

"Rachel! We have to get out of here! Can you get up?" Sylvia shouted desperately as she shook her friend.

Groggy, Rachel stirred. "What happened?" she asked, her voice thick with confusion.

Sylvia pulled Rachel out from under the spice shelf and helped her to her feet. "The store is on fire," Sylvia told her, terror in her voice. "Let's go!"

"My parents!" Rachel screamed, looking around in confusion. "Where are my parents? Mother! Papa!"

Sylvia, becoming stifled now and feeling the heat from the flames that were getting closer, grabbed Rachel's arm and pulled her, with great difficulty, toward the door. The entire store was ablaze. "We'll find them, Rachel! They're probably looking for us as well. Hurry! We gotta get out of here!"

Just as the terrified girls reached the door of the store, they heard Mr. Zucker's thick German accent outside, screaming for his daughter. "Rachel! Where is my Rachel!" he cried frantically.

Sylvia, still holding Rachel's arm, ran through the front door and outside into fresh, breathable air, and safety. Amazingly, the bell on the door still tinkled pleasantly.

Gasping and breathing hard, Sylvia looked at the gaping opening where the front glass window used to be, and watched Zucker's store burn. The new yellow paint on the front door bubbled and sizzled, melting any memories of the signs of hatred—those swastikas. Also ablaze was Miss Lillie's beloved little flower shop. The two businesses, once separated only by wooden walls, independent ownership, and mutual respect, now burned together in one incredible ball of flame and smoke, which snaked into the darkening sky. The outer walls of Mr. Crandall's barbershop, two doors down and separated from the others by an empty lot, stood smoke-blurred, but unharmed.

Rachel, safe in the arms of her parents, cried like a baby. Her mother, it turned out, had left the store to take out the trash and had found her husband wandering outside, screaming for his family.

By that time, the sirens of fire trucks and police cars began to pierce the sound of muffled explosions coming from the store as bags of goods were consumed. The air smelled of burned hair, smoldering leaves, and charred sugar. Dreams disappeared with the smoke.

Sylvia, standing off to one side by herself and shaking uncontrollably, was having trouble comprehending the enormity of what was happening. *This can't be real,* she thought, *not here in stupid old Little Rock.* Her pretty yellow dress, stained and torn in spots, hung on her like a wilted bloom. She wrapped her arms around herself and ached for her mother.

Bright orange and yellow flames tinged with blue drifted up

to the sky. The small stores, made mostly of thin plaster and wooden beams, were easy morsels for the fire to devour. It made no distinctions between bouquets of gardenias and shelves of oatmeal, between colorful carnations and bottles of syrup.

The two structures began to crumble in the heat. At one point two thin skeletons of wooden beams were perfectly outlined by the bright orange flames, an oddly beautiful painting of destruction. The fire hoses did little more than add decoration to the gloomy afternoon.

Mr. Crandall, his son Johnny, and the two Smith brothers stood quietly on the opposite corner, looking aghast at the destruction. Sylvia shivered. She did not see Miss Lillie at all. Finally, Crandall scratched his thinning hair, then walked across the street to where the Zucker family huddled together.

"Hey, Zucker. You all right?"

"Ya," Mr. Zucker replied shakily. "My family is safe. That is all that matters to me. What about you?"

"Fire didn't touch my shop." He shifted his weight from one foot to the other. "Hey, I know you and me got our differences, but I want you to know I never did nothing to hurt you."

"Ya. So you say." Mr. Zucker turned to hug his wife, then looked at Mr. Crandall with eyes filled with grief. "Thank you. Now go—we must deal with this tragedy ourselves, sir."

Mr. Crandall spat on the ground and walked away. "Can't even be nice to these folks," he mumbled.

People from all over the neighborhood, both colored and white, had gathered to watch the fiery show. Old women who had hurried from fixing their dinner, children who relished the spectacle of noise and excitement, men who had been cutting their grass—all rushed to the scene.

"I heard somebody say the stores got struck by lightning," one onlooker said.

"Wasn't no thunder or lightning within a hundred miles," another person said. "Somebody did this on purpose."

"Who would want to burn out old Zucker? He never hurt nobody. He lets folks shop on credit and his wife makes darn good cookies!"

"We got too many Jews in the neighborhood anyway!" another voice spat out.

"I heard Zucker supports the integrationists—those troublemakers from up north who are coming in here to upset our Negroes!" an indignant female voice said.

"We got plenty to be upset about, lady. We don't need no Northerners tellin' us how bad you be treatin' us," an angry Negro voice replied.

"I know plenty of folks who'd want to burn old Crandall to the ground! Seems kinda funny his shop didn't have a scratch on it," one man commented.

"Grady, quit talking like that," a woman's voice said. "We don't want to wish ill luck on nobody." The man said nothing else.

"What about sweet Miss Lillie?" a soft-spoken woman's voice said. "Nobody would want to hurt her, for sure."

"She took fresh flowers to Mrs. Z every morning," a woman said softly.

"Zucker's too friendly with the coloreds," another voice said into the gathering darkness. "Serves him right."

"Well, Crandall hates the coloreds and the Jews. Everybody knows that. Awfully strange he didn't get burned out."

"Seems like that fire don't care what color the owner used to be," a man's voice said harshly.

"Poor Miss Lillie," a woman added. "She loved that little shop."

"Miss Lillie must be the sweetest little colored lady in Little Rock," a white woman's voice said.

"Do they know who set the fire?" someone else asked.

"Not a clue. Any evidence probably got burned up."

"Such a shame. I'm going to miss those cookies."

"Anybody seen Miss Lillie?" another woman called out frantically. Only the silence of confusion answered.

Sylvia, still in shock, listened to the voices, but it was as if they were floating over her head. She didn't pay close attention to all the words.

She knew she had to call her mother, but she couldn't stop shaking. She walked over to where the Zuckers sat on the grass across the street from their store. Mrs. Zucker, who held Rachel in one arm, hugged Sylvia with her other, and for once her thick, enveloping embrace felt comforting. Sylvia huddled with them as they watched a lifetime go up in smoke.

FRIDAY, AUGUST 16, 1957—EVENING

Y ou saved my life," Rachel whispered finally.

Sylvia shook her head and managed a small chuckle. "I'm no hero. I saved *my* life—I just took you with me!"

"Ya, you save my Rachel," Mr. Zucker said thickly. "I can never thank you enough."

Sylvia felt uncomfortable and got shakily to her feet. Mrs. Zucker couldn't seem to stop crying.

"What will we do now, Papa?" Rachel asked her father.

"We do what we always do, my child. We go on." He scratched his forearm unconsciously.

As the ambulance drivers tended to Rachel's cuts and Sylvia's bruises, a police officer finally came over to where the Zucker family sat. "I'm really sorry about this, Mr. Zucker," the young policeman began, "but it looks like both buildings are going to be a total loss."

"That I can see," Mr. Zucker said without emotion.

"Do you have any idea how this might have started?" the policeman asked. "Any problems with wires or plugs or electric lights lately?"

Mr. Zucker looked up and laughed harshly. "In the past months I have had racial slurs and swastikas painted on my door on three separate occasions. I called the police each time. You come, you ask lots of questions, you take pictures, then you leave."

"Then what do you do, sir?" the policeman asked.

"I paint my door once more." Mr. Zucker stood up stiffly and looked at the young man face-to-face. "What do *you* do? Don't you think these incidents are related?"

"It could be random events, sir. We have no proof that those incidents are related to the fire, but we're going to do a thorough investigation."

"Investigate what?" Rachel asked angrily. "And how will

you find out who did this? Do you even care?" The officer looked away from her, scribbled on his clipboard, but did not reply.

"Is Miss Lillie all right?" Sylvia asked the policeman.

"We have not been able to locate her," he said with a bit of concern in his voice. "We hope she was out delivering flowers." He seemed to be glad to turn his attention away from the Zuckers for the moment.

"But she was in her window just a little while ago, working on her display," Sylvia said, fear in her voice.

"I'm sure she's fine—we'll keep you posted," the officer said. He hurried away, still writing notes on a clipboard.

Just then Sylvia's mother came running around the corner, her face a mask of fear and worry. Her bedroom slippers flopped crazily, and she had difficulty keeping them on as she ran. "Sylvie!" she screamed as she glanced with horror at the flames that greedily consumed the wooden frames of the buildings.

Sylvia jumped up and ran to her mother's arms. "Mama!" They reached each other in the middle of the street, which was blocked with fire hoses, emergency vehicles, and curious onlookers. Sylvia collapsed into tears at last, grateful for her mother's strong brown arms, the enormity of what had happened finally sinking in.

"I heard the sirens, but I ignored them at first. Then Gary ran in and told me it was Zucker's store, and I thought I had lost you!" her mother whispered into her ear.

"I should have called you right away, Mama, but the pay phone is a block away and my legs felt like they just wouldn't work. I'm sorry. I didn't mean to scare you."

"I'm just glad you weren't hurt. Are the Zuckers all right?" her mother asked, wiping her nose on a handkerchief. She glanced over at the trembling family on the grass. "What about Miss Lillie? Did the Crandalls get hurt? Oh, my Lord!" Mrs. Patterson covered her face and wept.

Sylvia had rarely seen her mother cry, and had never seen her out in public dressed as she was, wearing her old, torn bathrobe—the one she wore when she cleaned the oven—and her hair half in curlers, half-uncombed.

"It's okay, Mama," Sylvia said. "Rachel and her folks are fine—just a few cuts and bruises—they got out safely," Sylvia replied. "And, Mama, you look a mess!" Sylvia was grateful for the chance to smile.

Her mother wiped her eyes, pulled the remaining curlers out with one hand, and tucked them into the pocket of her bathrobe. A faint smile touched her lips. "First time in years I decide to get ready for bed early, and look what you make me do!" She took a deep breath, surveying the devastation. She did not let go of her daughter's hand. "Is everybody safe, Sylvie?" she asked.

"The Crandalls look okay—not a scratch on any of them. But nobody has seen Miss Lillie," Sylvia replied with concern.

Knocking down fire barriers and jumping over hoses, Calvin arrived with a clatter on his bicycle. "Where's my mother?" he shouted over the noise of the fire trucks and hoses. "Sylvie? Are you okay? Have you seen my mother?"

"I don't know, Calvin. Everything happened so fast." Sylvia looked distraught as Calvin ran toward the burning buildings.

"You can't go in there, son!" an officer yelled at Calvin, chasing him. "It's totally engulfed!"

Calvin ignored him and kept on running. The officer caught him and tackled him to the ground. Calvin squirmed and fought, but the policeman was stronger. "I gotta find her! I gotta find my mother!"

"If she's in there, you can't help her, son," the policeman said gently.

Finally, what was left of the two buildings, with a great whoosh, crumbled in on itself. The crowd stepped back in awe at the horror of it all. Sparks and flames flew into the sky, along with thick, black smoke. Calvin wept.

Sylvia and her mother walked over to where Calvin now sat on the sidewalk. Mrs. Patterson sat down on the ground, took the boy in her arms, and let him cry. Sylvia sat close by, afraid to think about what might have happened, or why.

When Calvin's grandfather arrived on the scene, they left the two of them huddled together, hoping for a miracle. But Calvin couldn't sit still. Restless, he walked aimlessly in front of the ruins, searching the faces in the crowd, looking in vain for his mother. He wasn't ashamed to let people see him cry. The firemen had set up ropes to hold the increasingly large crowd back—almost everybody in the neighborhood had ended up there, gawking at the tragedy that was unfolding in front of them.

Where's Reggie? Sylvia thought as her mind began to clear and she looked around at the huge throng of people. It seemed like everybody in Little Rock was out watching this, and Reggie was nowhere to be seen. Sylvia shuddered, trying to block out images she wanted desperately to forget.

Sylvia's father came speeding around the corner in the car a few minutes later, with a worried-looking Donna Jean and Gary in the backseat. They jumped out as one.

"Sylvia! What happened?" her father cried with anguish. "How did you get involved with this?"

Sylvia jumped up and grabbed her father. "Mama sent me to get some things so she could make cakes for the bake sale, Daddy. One minute I was talking to Rachel about the latest record on the radio, and the next thing I knew I was on the floor."

Her father embraced her tightly and whispered into her ear, "I love you, baby girl. Don't you dare go dyin' on me!"

Sylvia trembled in her father's arms, feeling incredibly safe enveloped in his words and the smell of his Old Spice cologne. "I'm okay, Daddy," she whispered. "Now that you're here, I know I'm gonna be all right."

DJ, standing alone on the sidewalk, shifted from one foot to the other. "I'm scared," she admitted.

Sylvia reluctantly left her father's reassuring arms and knelt down to give her sister a hug. "Me, too, DJ, but it's gonna be all right. Promise." She knew she sounded like her parents—lying about the truth to make the little ones feel safe.

The little girl trembled in her arms. "Was it those boys who knocked us down?" Donna Jean asked quietly. She barely blinked.

"What boys?" Mr. Patterson said, looking concerned.

"What are you talking about?" Mrs. Patterson asked, almost at the same time.

Sylvia bowed her head and wept once more. "I should have told you, Mama and Daddy. I'm so sorry. All of this is my fault!"

"You're not making any sense! Told us what? How could any of this possibly be your fault?" her father said.

Sylvia, her face streaked with dirt and tears, looked at her father. "A couple of months ago, when me and DJ went downtown to the library, Johnny Crandall and his friends the Smith brothers were kinda messing with us." She paused.

"Messing with you how? Tell me!" Her father sounded frantic.

"And you didn't tell me, Sylvie?" Her mother sounded hurt. "Come to think of it, you two did seem a bit subdued when you got home that day, as I remember now."

"I knew we should have told Mama," Donna Jean whispered to Sylvia.

"They didn't hurt us, Daddy. Not really. They yelled at us, kicked our books around, and pushed us down in the dirt." She paused. "Johnny Crandall slapped me. I was afraid to tell you." Sylvia made circles in the dirt with the toe of her shoe. *This is such a mess. I should have known better.*

"Slapped you! How dare he!" Mr. Patterson looked as if he were about to explode. He breathed heavily, unable to contain his frustration. He looked around wildly. For once, his face matched Gary's when he had reached a boiling point.

"That's why I didn't say anything, Daddy. I didn't want anything else bad to happen. It wouldn't have changed anything."

Her father sighed deeply. "So how does that incident have anything to do with this fire?"

"It's complicated." Sylvia knew she was stalling, but she didn't know what to say.

"Do you think the Crandall and Smith boys set the fire? Were they following you? Trying to hurt you?" She had never seen her father so upset. "I'm ready to smash my hand through this tree trunk, Sylvia! Please explain what you know." Mrs. Patterson touched her husband's arm, trying to calm him, but she looked worried as well.

Sylvia didn't have a chance to answer her father at that point, because the police walked over to interrogate her. After speaking to everyone in the Zucker family, and interviewing all the Crandalls, it was finally Sylvia's turn. She trembled with fear as the policeman approached.

"I need to ask you some questions," the young officer said to Sylvia. He had taken off his hat and his blond crew cut had taken the shape of the police cap.

"Can't I take her home first?" her mother asked. "She's injured and needs rest. Perhaps we can do this in the morning."

"This will only take a few minutes," the policeman replied.

"I'm okay, Mama. Let's get this over with," Sylvia said. But her hands were shaking.

"You were in Zucker's store when the fire began?" the officer asked. She wondered why the officer couldn't say "Mr. Zucker." The man had lost everything—surely he deserved a little respect.

She kept these thoughts to herself and replied respectfully, "Yes, sir. I was shopping for my mother."

"Do you often shop at Zucker's? There's a colored-owned store a couple of blocks away."

"Rachel Zucker is my friend, and the Zuckers are wonderful people. Our family has shopped there for years." *Why does everything boil down to race?* Sylvia thought angrily.

The policeman wrote down everything Sylvia said. "Did you see or hear anything unusual while you were shopping?"

"No. It all happened really fast. I heard breaking glass, then two thuds, then I smelled something oily—I guess it was kerosene—then smoke. I pulled myself and Rachel out of the building and watched it burn like everyone else."

"So you saw no one outside the building? No one running away?"

Sylvia hesitated. Her heart thudded. She wondered if the cop could see inside her, if he could tell whether she was telling the truth or not. "Uh, I was on the floor, and everything was kinda blurry."

"Think now. It's important."

"Uh, I did see someone's shoes."

"Could you tell whose feet they were? Was it a woman or a man?"

"A man."

"You're sure?"

"Women don't wear those kind of shoes," Sylvia said.

"Can you describe them?" the officer asked. He had not looked up from his clipboard.

"They were, uh, brown. And shiny. With pointy toes and laces. And taps. I'm sure I heard the taps as he walked." Chill bumps covered Sylvia's arms. She'd done it. Everybody in town knew Mr. Crandall's shoes.

The officer looked up with a start. "Are you sure, girl?"

Sylvia's mother also looked at her sharply. "Was it Mr. Crandall, Sylvia?" she asked carefully.

"Yes, Mama," Sylvia said, her head down.

"You're saying you saw Mr. Crandall in the store just as the explosions began?" the officer asked in disbelief.

"Yes, sir. I mean, I saw Mr. Crandall leaving the store after the explosions."

"Did you see or hear anyone else?"

Sylvia looked up at the sky. *Please forgive me, Lord.* "No, sir. That's all I saw."

The policeman wrote furiously on his clipboard, then hurried away to confer with the other officers. Sylvia watched them question the Crandalls again. Although she couldn't hear everything that was said, it was clear that Mr. Crandall was yelling, perhaps cursing, and was very, very angry. Sylvia felt lightheaded, like she might pass out.

The young officer returned to Sylvia, his face tight and angry. "How dare you lay blame on an upstanding citizen like Mr. Crandall?" he asked. "You almost made us arrest an innocent man!"

"I didn't accuse anybody," Sylvia replied shakily.

"She answered your questions and told you what she saw," Mrs. Patterson told the officer crisply as she moved closer to Sylvia.

"He said he went inside the store to make sure everyone got out safely. He's a hero, not a criminal!"

"He didn't save me," Sylvia replied quietly.

The policeman ignored her, but asked once more, "Are you sure you didn't see who tossed the firebombs, if that's what they were? Maybe you were just playing with matches and got careless!" He almost snarled at her.

"I told you everything I know. And I told the truth." Sylvia felt a deep pain in the pit of her stomach. *Oh, my Lord. What have I done?*

The officer gave Sylvia another sharp look, but said nothing else. Her father moved nearer to Sylvia and held her closely. Her thudding heartbeat was muffled by her father's large and comforting arms.

Mrs. Patterson walked over to the Zuckers then and sat down beside them on the grass. No one spoke. She placed her brown hand in Mrs. Zucker's pale one. The two of them sat there silently, hand in hand, watching the remains of the buildings sizzle and die. The water from the fire hoses drenched the already charred wood, but had had very little impact on the flames.

Just then a collective cheer erupted from the assorted onlookers as Miss Lillie's faded green 1951 Studebaker clattered around the corner. She jumped out and ran to Calvin and her father, who almost collapsed with relief. "I was out delivering flowers for the Nelson wedding," Sylvia heard her explain. "I heard about the fire on the car radio. We're gonna be okay, Calvin baby. We're gonna be just fine."

"Let's go home, Mama," Sylvia said, her eyes stinging with tears as well as smoke.

The Patterson family stepped over hoses and lines and ropes to get to their car, holding hands to steady one another. "I'm so glad Calvin will get to laugh again," Mrs. Patterson said. "The pursuit of happiness is the discovery of joy."

"Thanks, Mama. For once, I needed your little quote," Sylvia said as the Patterson family climbed into their car.

"I'm glad this is over," DJ said, relief in her voice.

Sylvia knew that the consequences of this day were far from complete. Her stomach ached with the knowledge.

Friday Night, August 16, 1957

I've never been up close to somebody dead. I was sure Miss Lillie had been killed, and just the thought made me feel ill—like I was about to throw up. Some friend I'd be—Calvin would be screeching and crying and needing somebody to turn to, and I'd be puking in the street. I'm so glad she's okay. If Mama died, I wouldn't know how to keep on breathing.

I still feel sick, but for a different reason. I've never lied to my parents before. For sure I've never lied to the police—never even had a conversation with a cop before. Yesterday I was a good girl who just wanted a boyfriend and a chance to make a difference in the world like everybody seems to think I ought to be doing. Today I'm a liar and a sinner and a criminal.

But it was all too much—the smoke, that smell, the way the ashes blew in the wind and landed on my head. I've never been so scared and so messed up inside. Johnny Crandall and his threats. Miss Lillie maybe gone forever. And Reggie—I've got to talk to him.

It never even occurred to me that it could have been me they were bringing out on a stretcher. All I could concentrate on was how bright the fire was, how hot the air felt, and how fast everything burned up and disappeared. Stuff they'd had their whole life—gone in just a short time.

Our house, standing there ugly and gray, was the most beautiful sight I'd ever seen when we pulled into the driveway. It seems like it would have changed while we were gone, like it should be feeling sad like we were, but instead it looked solid and safe.

I didn't realize how tired I was, or how sore. I was covered with eggs and spices, my hair was full of flour, my pretty yellow dress was filthy, and every muscle in my body ached. I couldn't get the smell of smoke and destruction out of my nostrils, or the image of those timbers glowing in the darkness. I took a shower and let the steamy water run over me for a long time. While no one could see me, I cried and cried and cried.

I cried for the Zuckers and all the Jewish people who had already suffered so much. I cried for Calvin and his mom and the loss of innocent little daisies in her shop. I cried for Miss Lillie, who was always nice to me. And I cried because I know the truth. What I don't know is why.

Why? Why? Why?

As I stepped out of the bathroom, still sniffling a little, Mama was there with a cup of hot tea—thick with lemon and honey like I like it. I sipped it while she brushed the tangles out of my hair. Words weren't necessary. Not yet.

SATURDAY, AUGUST 17, 1957

Sylvia awakened slowly, hoping the events of the night before had been just a horrible dream. Then she turned over, looked at the scratches on her arms, and knew it was all too real. Her throat felt raspy, and she still felt a little nauseous. She wondered why her body couldn't just shut down and let her sleep for a year or so.

She stretched and sat up, noticed her head ached a little, but she felt no serious aftereffects from the night before, at least not physically. She listened for the usual household sounds, but all seemed to be quiet downstairs. She noticed that Donna Jean had gotten up quietly and even made her own bed.

Sylvia got dressed, choosing a faded green dress that had been washed and worn so many times the fabric was soft. It made her feel safe. She took her time walking down the steps, each creak on the stair seeming to yell at her. Her family was just finishing breakfast. The room was unnaturally quiet—none of the usual arguing or laughter. "What's going on?" she asked quietly. She coughed and tried to shake away the thickness she felt.

Mr. Patterson sat quietly, sipping his coffee, a slight frown on his face.

"Drink some of this orange juice, Sylvia," her mother said with concern. "You sound a little parched."

"Thanks, Mama, but I'm not very hungry this morning."

"But I saved you two strips of bacon," Donna Jean offered, her eyes large with concern.

"That was nice of you, DJ," Sylvia managed to say. "Maybe later." Just looking at the food made her choke.

Gary, unusually silent, crumbled a biscuit into little pieces. Finally, he looked up and asked Sylvia, "You talk to Reggie lately?"

Startled, Sylvia said, "Uh, no, not for a couple of days."

Gary said nothing else, but continued to play with his food.

Sylvia felt weak at the stomach, afraid to think that Gary could somehow have been involved in this mess as well.

"Rachel called first thing this morning," Mrs. Patterson said as she wiped invisible crumbs from the table. "She said to tell you they're staying with relatives for now. And she said to tell you thanks once more."

Sylvia nodded and shrugged. "I'm just glad nobody got hurt."

"One of the ladies from the church called to say that Calvin and his mother are with Miss Lillie's father," her mother continued.

The whole day before spun through Sylvia's mind, and she reeled from the images. She ran to her mother, who let her cry into her apron.

Her father reached over and gently touched Sylvia on the shoulder. "Do you feel like talking, Sylvie?" His voice, filled with understanding, was softer than she'd ever heard it.

Sylvia gulped, wiped her eyes, and nodded. "Are you gonna be mad at me, Daddy?"

"Of course not, child. What could you possibly have done to make me angry?"

Sylvia said nothing at first. "I didn't tell the police everything," she admitted slowly.

"What did you leave out? Do you know who set the fires?" Her father had placed his coffee cup back on the saucer. The rest of the family was silent.

"Well, first I saw some shoes. They were brown, shiny oxfords with metal taps on the toes and the heels. I could hear them click."

"So it *was* Crandall after all!" her father gasped.

"No, Daddy. Mr. Crandall was in the store, but I think it was like he said—he had heard glass breaking or something, and he came in to see what was going on. He didn't bother to help anybody—he ran out when he saw what had happened—but he didn't do it."

"Are you sure?" her mother asked, sounding confused.

"I think so, Mama."

"Then who did it?" her father insisted.

Sylvia gulped and trembled. "Well, I'm not sure, but I think I saw . . ."

The shrill ringing of the doorbell made the whole family jump with apprehension. "I'll get it," Gary said as he strode across the room. When he opened the door, Sylvia gasped. Walking into her living room was Reggie.

For months Sylvia had been dreaming of asking her mother if Reggie could come over one Sunday for dinner. She'd planned it all in her mind—she'd be wearing her best dress, her hair would be combed just perfect, and they'd have fried chicken and baked potatoes and maybe an apple pie that she had baked herself. Never did she think he'd show up like this—with her looking a mess and him looking worse. Nothing was as it should be.

Reggie stood in the middle of the living room, head down. His raggedy blue tennis shoes were covered with dried mud, his shirt was wrinkled and ripped, and his slacks were filthy. "Excuse me, Pastor Patterson, sir, and Mrs. Patterson, ma'am," he said awkwardly. "Forgive me for interrupting your breakfast, but I came to ask if I could speak to Sylvia just for a moment. It's kinda important."

Her father cleared his throat, frowned, but nodded. "Do you need help, young man?"

"I'll be fine, sir," Reggie replied politely. "But I gotta talk to Sylvia—please."

"Does this have anything to do with you, Gary?" Mr. Patterson asked then.

"Believe it or not, Dad," Gary said, holding up his arms, "I'm not part of this one." Mr. Patterson looked relieved.

Donna Jean watched the whole scene, wide-eyed.

Mrs. Patterson asked Reggie, "Are you hungry, son? I can scramble a couple of eggs real quick if you'd like." *Always the perfect hostess,* Sylvia mused, *even in the middle of a catastrophe!*

"Thank you, ma'am, but I can't. Is it all right if I talk to Sylvia on the porch?"

Sylvia looked at her mother, who nodded and said, "Put a sweater on before you go out, Sylvie." Sylvia recognized the all-knowing look on her mother's face. "But don't be long. We're in the middle of something important here."

"Yes, Mama," Sylvia replied faintly. She grabbed a sweater from the coatrack and ran outside before her parents could say anything else. Reggie followed behind her, glancing back at Gary before he closed the front door.

The two of them stood there on her porch for a moment, just looking at each other, saying nothing.

"Walk with me a little," Reggie said shakily. The steps creaked as they left the porch.

"The air still smells like smoke," she said softly as she took a deep breath of the morning air.

Reggie paused, then shuddered. "Nobody in town knows who really caused the fire."

"I do," Sylvia said quietly.

"What?"

"I saw you, but I didn't tell the police."

"You lied? For me?"

"I didn't lie. I just didn't tell the whole truth, which I guess is just as bad. I feel dirty inside."

"I'm so sorry, Sylvie—for everything." Tears trickled down his face.

"Why, Reggie? Why did you do it? I don't get it."

The morning sun shone as if the day held hope and promise, but all was dark in Sylvia's mind. Reggie took her hand and cried unashamedly. Finally, he gulped, sniffed, and wiped his face with the back of his shirtsleeve. "I never meant to hurt anybody, Sylvie. The Zuckers have always been cool to me, and Calvin's mom has always been as sweet to me as if I were her own son. She always smells good." He sniffed, trying not to break down again.

"Tell me everything," Sylvia said.

Reggie started walking again, as if it were easier for him to talk as he moved. "I think about you all the time, Sylvia," he began. "I dream about you at night." He looked over at her and smiled sadly.

The words she'd always wanted to hear, but not like this. This was such a mess. "Oh, Reggie," she said sadly.

"When you told me how you and your sister got pushed around by the Crandall boy and the Smith brothers, I wanted to make them pay for hurting you." He looked over at Sylvia again. "It was all for you."

"I still don't understand what happened," she said, feeling guilty.

"Johnny Crandall and his friends hang out at his father's shop every Friday after school. Sometimes I have to walk home that way, and they always yell at me and call me names. I'd had just about enough, but when they messed with you, that was the last straw. So I thought about it for a long time, and I decided to make a couple of firebombs." He waited.

"You what?! How do you even know how to make such a thing?"

"Well, you know those meetings I've been going to with Gary?"

She nodded, amazement on her face. She removed her hand from Reggie's.

"Some of the older guys are radical—they talk about violent protests, not the stuff Dr. King preaches. One of the guys talked about how to make firebombs."

"Gary's been making bombs?" Sylvia asked, astonished.

"No, I'm the stupid one, not him." Reggie hung his head again. "They were just supposed to be little puffs of smoke and fire to scare the Crandalls—nothing dangerous. I must have made them too powerful."

"I can't believe you were walking down the streets of Little Rock with firebombs in your hands. It sounds like something out of a movie or TV show." Sylvia shuddered.

"Except it's real life, and I'm a big chicken," he said. "I didn't have the courage to toss them. I had just about decided to go back home when I saw that punk Johnny harassing you again. It made me nuts."

"You were there and didn't say anything?" Sylvia felt like her head was going to burst.

"I had two firebombs under my shirt. I couldn't come up to you and act normal. As soon as I saw that Johnny was in the barbershop, I decided to toss what I thought would be something like firecrackers. "

"But Crandall's barbershop wasn't harmed," Sylvia said, still confused.

"Remember last year when I didn't make the baseball team?" Reggie asked.

"Yeah."

"It was because I couldn't throw worth a darn. Coach said I had *really* bad aim." He paused. "I aimed for the barbershop, but the firebomb hit Zucker's window instead. I went crazy because I knew you were in there."

"Oh, Reggie." It was all so pathetic.

"I ran into the store to get you out and dropped the second bomb accidentally when I slipped on something that had spilled. I got scared because I couldn't see you. Everything was smoke and fallen stuff. Then Mr. Crandall came in and I ran out the back door. I panicked. I had no idea the fire would be so big. No idea."

"I tried to cry out when I saw you, but I couldn't. I could hardly breathe, " she said sadly, remembering it clearly. "I could have died." The thought made her dizzy.

He looked directly at Sylvia. "I'm so sorry. I didn't know what to do." He dropped his eyes. "I'm the one who deserves to die."

She frowned. "It was stupid, Reggie. Really stupid. But you didn't mean for any of this to happen."

"But it did." He scowled. Reggie gazed down Sylvia's street—the neat little houses, the crooked sidewalks, the morning sun on the tiny, well-kept lawns. "I love Little Rock," he said wistfully.

"You have to make this right, Reggie." Sylvia sighed, knowing that things had forever changed between them. "Somehow you have to fix what you messed up."

"I don't know what to do," he said helplessly. "Maybe I ought to just leave town like my dad says. I've got relatives in

Cincinnati. If I stay, I'll go to jail. I'm not scared to face my punishment, but I can't help anybody if I'm locked up."

The thought of Reggie in jail made her head swim, but the idea of him cutting out on his responsibility made her ill. "You can't run away from this," she said. "That really would be the coward's way out."

"I'll be back one day," he said vaguely. "But not until I make my parents, and you, proud of me again. I'm going to get a job—maybe two jobs, and I swear, even if it takes a hundred years, I swear I'll pay them for what they lost." For the first time, Sylvia noticed, he held his head a little higher. "I promise on my life."

"It wasn't supposed to be like this," Sylvia said sadly. "I had such stupid teenaged dreams about you and me. Lace curtains and picket fences and flowers in a garden someplace in a make-believe world. You've spoiled it, you know."

"Yeah, I know. But those dreams weren't stupid," he told her, his face drawn and serious. "It's just that the real world isn't as pretty as we hoped."

"But we can try to make it better," Sylvia insisted. "Come in the house and talk to my dad," she said. "He might be able to figure something out."

"Oh, I couldn't. I'd be ashamed to face him." Reggie turned away from her.

"Be a man, Reggie!" Sylvia's eyes flashed with anger. "The whole town is going to know what you did very soon. There might be a better solution than running away with your tail tucked. White folks expect the worst from us anyway. Don't give them the satisfaction of being right."

Monday Night, August 19, 1957

Daddy is a miracle worker. He convinced Reggie to confess to the police, and apologize to the Zuckers and the Cobbs. They aren't pressing charges, but Reggie still has been charged with vandalism. Daddy says he'll be tried in juvenile count, and he'll probably only have to do community service, or pay something toward the damage. He'll have to drop out of school, for now, at least, I suppose. I've never known a dropout. I always thought they were bad kids who got in fights and skipped school and made bad grades. Not kids like Reggie who I've known all my life.

He has already promised to work and give his paycheck to the two families every week. Like his little dollar-an-hour job is going to make a difference! They've got lives to rebuild. Reggie can't pay for that. It's amazing how families in the neighborhood, both colored and white, are kicking in to help them rebuild. Mr. Herman from the hardware store gave them lumber; Mr. Massey from the dry goods store offered paint; and women from all over have been taking the two families food. That makes me feel good, especially with all the ugliness still burning in the city. The Mothers' League is still stirring up hatred, and the newspaper is still printing articles that predict World War Three if integration happens.

The past two nights I've had terrible dreams about the fire and explosions, about how close I came to death. Everything was so hot, so very red. It's like my brain is full of color and smoke. I wake up screaming and Mama comes in to soothe me.

Reggie is out of my life. I won't be seeing him anymore. That hurts, but only a little. Too much real pain floating around. I want to feel sorry for him, but he went too far. I finally get a boyfriend and he turns out to be all mixed up. Maybe Rachel was right—he was just training wheels for the real thing. All I know is I have a big burning hole inside of me. I feel like a dancer with no partner.

dance with me my agony
brittle on a shelf
dance beyond my misery
lost within myself

tears and pain tears and pain
memories return
dancers never leave the stage
fires always burn

dance away dance away
dance away from fear
spin around spin around
spin and disappear

mama! mama! hug me quick!
i dreamed you flew away!
you perched on the back
of a large green bird
with feet like clumps of clay

mama! mama! hug me tight!
and wake me from my sleep!
you smile as i dance
to a dark stale song
and tears like mud i weep

mama! mama! hug me now!

i dreamed of shadows past
you watched as i burned
in the cold dark fire
like hope that could not last

WEDNESDAY, AUGUST 21, 1957

Dressed that morning in a new blue and white sailor-styled blouse and navy blue skirt, Sylvia felt refreshed. Her mother, who always sensed exactly what her children needed, knew that for once, homemade wouldn't do. Instead of making the outfit on her sewing machine, she had brought it home from the department store and left it on Sylvia's bed the night before.

"Thanks, Mama," Sylvia said with pleasure as she twirled around in the full skirt in her parents' bedroom. "It's beautiful!"

"It's a back-to-school outfit," her mother replied, her tone practical, but she smiled as she said it. "Don't get it mussed and dirty before the first day. You're going to school with white children—I expect you to act as pretty as you look."

The thought of going to Central made the sunny day seem suddenly cloudy, but Sylvia refused to focus on that today. "You know I'll always do my best to make you proud, Mama," Sylvia said, sitting on the edge of her mother's bed.

"You always do, child. Maybe I don't tell you often enough how proud I am of you." She reached over and squeezed Sylvia's shoulder. "You shine in school, and you make good decisions, even if they're difficult sometimes. Sometimes my heart can't hold all the joy you bring me."

Sylvia glanced at her mother and was amazed to see she was blinking away tears. She shifted on the bed, unused to emotion from her strong, practical mother. "Can I ask you something, Mama?" Sylvia asked softly.

"Of course." Her mother got up, sniffed, and fluffed a pillow.

Sylvia took a deep breath. "Reggie looked like a piece of carved chocolate candy to me. The sound of his voice made me shiver. He even *smelled* like something good enough to lick off a plate. So if I'm so smart, why couldn't I figure out he was just a piece of cardboard?"

Her mother laughed out loud. "Oh, Sylvie, women have been asking that question since Adam and Eve! It sometimes takes a lifetime to figure out men. You're young—you've got plenty of time to find the right one for you." She gave her daughter another squeeze. "Any man who wins your heart is a lucky fellow, you hear me?"

"How did you know you were in love with Daddy?" Sylvia dared to ask. She didn't want anything to disturb this moment of closeness with her mom.

"It happened two weeks after our wedding day."

"After you got married?"

"Well, I knew he was special, and I knew I cared about him deeply—deep enough to promise the rest of my life to him, but love is not bells and flowers and a pretty white dress. It's something deeper."

"I don't get it." Sylvia was fascinated.

"We'd been married two weeks and it was pouring rain that day. I was on the bus, coming home from work, and all I had on was my new pink cotton dress. I didn't have a coat or umbrella or hat. We lived in a tiny apartment three blocks from the bus stop. I just knew I'd be soaked by the time I got home."

"So what happened?"

"As the bus approached my stop, I could see your father standing there, sopping wet, with a puppy-dog grin on his face, holding a big black umbrella, a shiny yellow raincoat, and a bouquet of red roses. It was then that I knew I loved him. And that he loved me."

"Wow. That's a really good story. Why haven't you told me before?"

"I don't know. You were too young to understand, I guess."

Sylvia almost didn't recognize the soft, dreamy woman who was smoothing the covers on the bed. Surely this couldn't be her prim and proper mother. Sylvia wished this conversation could last forever. "Did you and Daddy meet at church?" she asked.

Her mother laughed. "I never told you where I first met your father?"

Sylvia shook her head. Her parents rarely talked about their youthful years. All Sylvia knew of her parents' marriage was the black-and-white photo on the mantel. It showed two serious-looking younger versions of her parents standing stiffly in her grandmother's living room. Her mother, slim and smooth-cheeked, dressed in a high-necked, white lace dress, stood next to a very slim young man with dark, curly hair and a look of fierce determination on his face.

"I met him at a jitterbug contest!" Sylvia's mother admitted with a grin.

"You're kidding!" Sylvia almost fell off the bed.

"I was sixteen, and he was the best dancer in the county. All the girls wanted to take a spin on the dance floor with that handsome hunk, Lester Patterson."

Sylvia couldn't picture it. Not her solid serious father. "Grandma let you go to a dance contest?" Sylvia asked incredulously.

"I was supposed to be at the library, but Bessie let me tag along that night. Even she wasn't supposed to be there, but she was older and always has been the saucy one. Grandma would have killed us both if she had known." She chuckled at the memory.

The image of her mother being a teenager and sneaking into dance halls was almost too much for Sylvia to handle. "Did Grandma ever find out?"

"Yes, eventually. Mothers have a way of always figuring out everything. But by that time he was courting me proper, and coming to church with me every week. Grandma was crazy about him. She told me, 'That boy is more than breath and britches, Leola. Hang on to him.' She was right."

"When I find a boy like that, will you tell me?" Sylvia asked.

"Absolutely! I guarantee to make sure you know my opinion on every young man who shows an interest in you from now on."

"I shoulda kept my mouth shut," Sylvia said with a grin, feeling easy and comfortable with her mother for a change. "Not that there's much chance of me finding a boyfriend at Central," she added ruefully.

"You're going to school to learn, not find a husband," her mother replied, a briskness returning to her voice. "I want you to stand tall, walk with dignity, and feel the pride the whole community carries for you."

"Not everybody thinks this integration stuff is a good idea," Sylvia said carefully.

"You have to live by your own set of standards, Sylvia. You can't let others make decisions for you." Mrs. Patterson tidied up the room as they talked, picking up her husband's socks and tossing them into a laundry hamper.

"I feel so stupid sometimes—like I'm walking around knee-deep in mud and haven't got sense enough to get out of the cornfield."

"Like I've been trying to tell you—your father and I were young once, Sylvia. And we made lots of mistakes. Your road is not an easy one. Nobody expects you to travel it perfectly."

"It's hard to imagine you and Daddy as ever being young and foolish. I figured you just appeared one day, fully grown and knowing all the answers," she teased.

"I was silly and headstrong like you can be sometimes, and your father was very much like Gary—always conscious of insults and discrimination. Your father rarely did more than complain, however. Gary's got more guts."

"What about DJ?" Sylvia longed to keep her mother talking.

"She's a great mix of both of us—opinionated and outspoken, but needing constant reassurance that she's on the right track. She'll be the lawyer of the family."

"We'll probably need her to get Gary out of jail one day!" Sylvia said, only half-joking.

Mrs. Patterson sighed. "I hope not. Maybe this whole situation with the fire has calmed Gary down a little."

"Would you be disappointed in me if I ran away from all this racial confusion and joined the circus?" Sylvia asked.

"Now your brother I'd almost expect to see on the back of a decorated elephant," her mother replied with a smile. "But I would expect you to be in the front office of the circus, running the show and collecting ticket money. You're just that kind of young woman, Sylvia."

"What's this I hear about a circus?" Gary asked as he popped his head in the bedroom door.

"Want to run away with me to perform for Barnum and Bailey?" Sylvia asked. "I hear they have openings for flamethrowers and trapeze artists. We could be a dynamic duo!"

"Would Mama come with us?" Gary asked with a grin.

"What's the sense of running away from home if you take your mother with you?" Sylvia asked, feeling silly.

"Well, who would fix us blueberry muffins every morning?" He strode across the room and enveloped his mother in a bear hug.

"Quit, boy," she replied, but it was clear she was enjoying the moment.

He released his mother and looked at Sylvia. "I'd love to run away with you, kid, but I gotta stay here in stupid old Little

Rock. This is my senior year and I'm gonna fool everybody by settling down and graduating!"

Mrs. Patterson beamed. "That makes me real happy, Gary."

"I know, Mama. But I'm still gonna keep an eye on Sylvie and all the folks who plan to use violence to stop integration. I'm not going to let anybody at Central hurt her. The circus might need her one day." He winked at his sister.

In spite of the lightness of the conversation, every time the mention of Central High School came up in conversation, Sylvia felt the mud thicken around her.

FRIDAY, AUGUST 23, 1957

The weather had been amazingly hot and humid all week. Sylvia and DJ took turns trying to cool each other with a cardboard church fan, but all it did was stir the hot air around their faces.

After dinner, when the family was well-fed and relaxed, Sylvia decided it was time to tell them her decision. She smiled to herself, marveling over how many important discussions in their family were settled over plates of macaroni and roast beef. *It's a good thing we eat so much—we'd never get anything figured out in this family otherwise!*

"I'm going to call Miss Daisy Bates this afternoon," Sylvia began without introduction, "and have my name removed from the list of students who will integrate Central High School."

"I'm glad," DJ whispered.

Sylvia's mother moved next to her daughter and hugged her.

"You know you've got your family behind you, no matter what you decide."

"I know, Mama," Sylvia said, her shoulders shaking.

"Did Reggie have something to do with your decision?" Gary asked.

"Probably a little. But this is about me, not Reggie."

"You know you're smart enough and brave enough, and probably even cute enough to make it at Central," Gary teased. "Are you sure you want to drop off the list?"

"Yeah, I'm sure." Sylvia looked at her brother, her head tilted to one side. "You know, Gary, although I really wanted *you* to be the one they chose, there's a reason they didn't ask you to be one of the students to go to Central."

Gary started pacing, his long legs striding nervously across the floor. He grabbed the broom from his mother and started sweeping. "I know. Too hotheaded for my own good," he mumbled over the swooshes of the broom.

"Reggie looked up to you and your friends. He wanted to be like you—a quick-change artist of problems that have been around for hundreds of years. I don't think he was ready for the big time. He's just a kid."

"Is Reggie still your boyfriend?" DJ asked.

Sylvia smiled sadly. "I guess he'll always be my very first love. But he can't be my today love. It's not like in the songs on *American Bandstand*, DJ. Sometimes love gets all messed up."

"That's the saddest thing I ever heard," DJ said wistfully.

"But I'm not leaving the list because my boyfriend was the one who tried to burn down Little Rock. It's because of me. I'm not the person I thought I was. I'm not brave and noble, like everybody seems to think." She took the broom from her brother. It gave her something to do.

"What do you mean, Sylvia?" her father asked. "Nobody could ask for a finer young lady than you—you're smart and pretty and poised and confident. Those Central people couldn't find a better prospect than my Sylvia," he said with sincerity.

"Thanks, Daddy. That means so much to me."

"So what's the real reason you're not going to try to be one of the integrators, Sylvia? Is it because of the fire? Because of people like the Crandalls?" Her father leaned forward in his chair.

Sylvia took a deep breath and leaned on the broom. "I almost died in that fire. Even though I was really scared, I found out I'm not afraid to die, which really surprised me. And I'm not afraid of the Crandalls or people like them. What terrified me when I was lying on that floor is that I'd never get the chance to learn what I needed to learn, never have the time to do what I needed to do."

Her father beamed. "That's my girl! You've been paying attention to my sermons, haven't you?"

"Not really, Daddy," Sylvia admitted with a chuckle.

"I don't get it," DJ said.

"I need what the colored school will give me for the next four years. I have to suck up as much pride and dignity as I can while it's there for me. Integration will happen eventually, and we're gonna lose something when it does—that feeling of being special when we walk in the school yard because it's just us."

"Isn't that what I've been saying all along?" DJ screeched.

"Nobody listens to me!" She rolled her eyes dramatically and flopped on the sofa.

"I hear you, little sis," Gary said. "I just don't pay any attention to you!" He tossed a sofa pillow at her.

Sylvia smiled at them, then continued. "I want to go to college. I want to be a teacher like Miss Washington—only with better clothes," she added with a laugh, "so little colored girls like me can grow up proud of their brown skin and fuzzy hair. I don't think I can suck that in like I need to from teachers and kids at an all-white high school."

"What about the kids who *are* going to go?" Gary asked.

"I'm behind them one hundred percent! For them, it's the right thing to do right now."

Sylvia's mother, weeping softly, hugged her daughter once more. "I've never been so proud of you, Sylvie."

Sylvia pulled away. "Thanks, Mama, but I did some stuff I'm not proud of last week. I lied to the police. I'm not so great." She glanced at Gary.

"You didn't lie, Sylvie. You just left out some of the truth. I would have done the same thing," Gary insisted.

"Yeah, but this is me, not you. You still want to fight and protest."

"True, but I've given up firebombs!" Gary said with a wry smile.

"I guess we can thank Reggie for that," Sylvia replied, smiling back at her brother. "But I have to feel good about myself when I look in the mirror. I like feeling proud, and last week I didn't."

"Nonsense," her mother said. "That was a day of incredible

stress and trauma. Trespasses are forgiven with each dawn. Tuck that in your heart, you hear."

Sylvia nestled close to her mother, and they joined DJ on the sofa.

"Mama?" DJ asked.

"What, sweetie?"

"Can we take the plastic off the sofas and sit on the real fabric just once before we die?"

The whole family laughed heartily then. Gary ran over and started tickling his two little sisters, and their parents joined in—all five of them rolling on the living room floor.

Saturday, August 31, 1957

School starts next week, but it's not going to be the same. Not having Reggie around is like having one of my legs cut off—everything is all crooked. Now that I don't have the Central decision to worry about and think about, I feel lighter—like a bowling ball is gone out of my lap, but heavier, too, because I feel like I let them down.

I found out that seven other kids from the seventeen that had met at Daisy Bates's house back in June had also withdrawn from the list. Some decided they wanted to be able to participate in activities. Some had parents who were scared. One moved away, I think. That leaves just nine students to try to integrate Central High School. All of them excel in academics, sports, music, and service.

Ernest Green is the oldest and will be entering Central as a senior. He'd been in the National Honor Society at Mann, played the tenor saxophone, and he was an Eagle Scout. He'll be giving up a lot by letting go of his senior year with friends he'd been in school with since kindergarten. Jefferson Thomas, a track star, and Carlotta Walls, active in the National Junior Honor Society and the Student Council, are the youngest and will be entering as tenth graders. Gloria Ray, Melba Pattillo, Minnijean Brown, Terrence Roberts, Thelma Mothershed, and Elizabeth Eckford will be juniors.

I'm scared for them. I envy them.

MONDAY, SEPTEMBER 2, 1957

It was Labor Day, the last official day of summer. It was traditionally a time for picnics and hot dogs and watermelon, for children to play hopscotch and jacks, and for teenagers like Sylvia to plan what to wear on the first day of high school. But here in Little Rock, most of the Negro families stayed in their homes, talking in hushed voices, worrying about what would happen the following morning.

"Governor Faubus has called out the Arkansas National Guard," her mother told Sylvia as she got out of bed.

"Why?" Sylvia asked sleepily. "We got soldiers marching in the streets of Little Rock? That's crazy."

"He says it's 'to preserve the peace and avert violence,' but it seems to me he's asking for trouble." Her mother, of course, had a broom in her hand and was sweeping the floor furiously.

"Has anybody threatened anything violent?" Sylvia asked her, dodging the broom so it wouldn't sweep over her toes. Aunt Bessie had told Sylvia once that it was bad luck if somebody brushed over a person's feet. She never told her what would happen—Sylvia figured she didn't know herself.

"Not that I've heard of. It's like the governor is creating a monster and it's getting bigger and stronger every day."

Later that evening the monster grew uglier and more frightening. Sylvia and her family watched in silence as the governor came on television and announced that he had called out the National Guard "to prohibit the nine black students from entering Central High School." He said that he had received warnings about "caravans of automobiles, filled with white supremacists," which were headed toward Little Rock.

"Is he making this up as he goes?" Gary asked, his mouth open in disbelief.

"Do you think it's true?" Sylvia asked him fearfully.

"What's true is that Faubus is the king of all racists, and he's feeding the fear of lots of folks who wouldn't like integration but wouldn't have the nerve to try to stop it."

They listened quietly to the rest of the governor's speech. He also declared Horace Mann School off-limits to whites. Gary and Sylvia laughed out loud at that. "Ha!" Gary snorted. "Fat chance of any white kids hanging around our school anyway!"

Governor Faubus ended his speech by saying "blood will run in the streets" if black students should try to enter Central High School. Gary and Sylvia stopped laughing.

TUESDAY, SEPTEMBER 3, 1957

It was the first day of school. "I have to leave early, Sylvia," her mother said as she put on a pearl earring. "Donna Jean! Get your shoes on and let's go. The children at school are going to need me today—I don't want them to be any more frightened than necessary. Several of them have brothers or sisters who are heading to Central today." She grabbed DJ's lunch and her school bag and hurried out the door. "Come on, Lester! Hurry up!"

Mr. Patterson grinned at Sylvia and gulped the last of his coffee. "Don't mess with a woman wearing pearls! I'll be right back," he said, "to take you and Gary over to Mann."

Gary, already dressed, sat in the living room, mesmerized by the events unfolding on the television screen. "Come here, Sylvie," he said. "You're not gonna believe this."

Sylvia flopped down on the sofa, careful not to wrinkle her new dress, and watched in amazement while the camera panned the vastness of Central High School, huge and imposing, taking up a whole city block. "It looks like a castle or a fortress—all brick and brown and solid."

"Yeah. Like something out of a history book," Gary said.

Sylvia shuddered because today, on the front steps, and in front of the huge front doors, stood soldiers, dressed in dull green. "It's like watching a movie, Gary," Sylvia said in sad horror. "Only this is very live and very real, happening right here in Little Rock, just a few blocks from our house."

"I want to be out there with them," he replied passionately. "I want to stand up for my people, fight for my rights!"

"Gary!" she shrieked. "They've got guns!"

"Yeah, they do. With real bullets."

"Who are they gonna shoot—the kids who try to integrate, or the protesters?"

"I have no idea."

Hundreds of white students nervously approached their

school with what Sylvia knew was more than the normal worries about the first day of the school year. Instead of the usual noise and laughter that you'd expect from teenagers, it was eerily silent. But every single white student entered the front door with no problem.

"Where are the Negro students?" their father asked when he returned.

"We haven't seen any yet," Gary told his father. Mr. Patterson, instead of rushing Gary and Sylvia to school, sat down in the living room and watched the unbelievable scene with them.

A reporter stopped a few students and interviewed them as they climbed the steps to enter the building. "What do you think about the National Guard being at your school?" a female student was asked.

"I think they're cute!" she replied. "It's exciting they're here, and it makes me feel safe."

"What do *you* think about integration?" the reporter asked a young man.

"I think it's fine, but I think the coloreds are rushing it too much. They should wait until next year—by then I'll have graduated!" He laughed and walked into the building.

A dark-haired young woman walked up the steps next. Sylvia gasped as she recognized the girl immediately.

"Daddy! It's Rachel Zucker! Wait till she finds out she's been on television. She'll be so excited."

"Do you have any comments to make on this historic day?" the reporter asked Rachel, thrusting the microphone in front of her.

"I would like to see a world where no hatred exists," she said clearly. She then marched past him.

"Hah!" Gary laughed. "I bet the reporter didn't like that answer!"

"He had no idea what Rachel's been through in the past few weeks. I'm proud of her," Sylvia said.

Another reporter came on camera and stated, with excitement in his voice, "The Mothers' Coalition held a sunrise service this morning, right here at the school." Sylvia figured he was hoping something horrible or exciting would happen. Reporters seemed to like bad news. He continued, "About two hundred people attended. They sang 'Dixie,' raised the Confederate battle flag, and praised Faubus's speech."

Sylvia's father grunted at that and stood up. "Let's get you two to school. I'm more glad than ever that neither of you are in that group. For some reason I seem to prefer my children safe and not bleeding all over the carpet."

"I'm willing to bleed, Dad," Gary reminded him.

"I know you are, son. We just want to see you safely to graduation. Don't try to save the world for a while, you hear? And don't you dare go over to that school!" Gary grabbed his books, but said nothing in response.

School was hot, crowded, and, in spite of all the tension in the rest of the city, actually fun for Sylvia. She liked her teachers, her classes looked as if they were going to be challenging like she liked them to be, and she knew most of the students. Everything just felt *right*.

"Hey, Sylvia," Calvin said, coming up behind her and tickling her.

"Hey, yourself. How's your mom?"

"She's started selling flowers out of Grandpa's house now,

so the living room is stuffed with carnations and tulips, and the bathroom is full of roses. Really rough when you have to use the toilet!" He made a face.

Sylvia laughed. "I'm glad things are bouncing back a little."

"Do you know Reggie has already started sending money to us? Mama didn't think he would, but an envelope with a few dollars has come every week since he left."

"I'm glad," Sylvia replied. "Tell your mother if there's anything she needs, just call me."

"Speaking of needy women," Calvin said with a grin, "if you ever need somebody to lean on, I'm your man," Calvin told her. "Just don't ask to use my bathroom!" He laughed and ran to his next class.

Sylvia couldn't believe that her life was so pleasant right now, while nine of her friends had to be biting their fingernails to the bone, worrying about what would happen. That's all the teenagers at Mann talked about at lunch.

"I think they ought to leave well enough alone and wait until things calm down a little before they try to integrate," Lou Ann said.

"How long? Another hundred years?" a big football player named Edwin answered with a jeer.

"I don't see *you* out there signing up to go!" Lou Ann reminded him. He said nothing more.

"White folks always get what they want. It's gonna get ugly out there if those nine kids try to buck the governor," a girl named Lizzie said.

"You get the idea the nine of them are being used by the political folks?" Lou Ann asked.

"I feel sorry for them," Candy Castle said. She wore a surprisingly simple navy blue dress that was not tight or revealing. *Maybe she's changed,* Sylvia noted.

"I'm scared for them," Sylvia said quietly. Most kids murmured agreement.

"Are you glad you're no longer on the list?" Lou Ann asked Sylvia.

"A little." Sylvia's stomach churned. "I feel guilty, though, like I gave up—not on me, but on them."

"Well, it starts tomorrow," Lou Ann said. "Miss Daisy is a friend of my mother, and she told her they would finally try tomorrow."

"Are the soldiers there to help them go in or to keep them out?"

"I think the governor plans to keep them out," Lou Ann replied solemnly.

WEDNESDAY, SEPTEMBER 4, 1957

Donna Jean has a bad cold, Sylvia Faye. Do you think you could stay home with her today?"

"Mama!" Sylvia protested. "It's the second day of school! No fair!"

"She's sneezing, she's got a temperature, and I just can't stay with her—not today. You know I never ask you to do this, but it's an emergency."

"What about Gary?"

"He left early, and your father has a prayer meeting with the rest of the preachers in town. I gave DJ a couple of baby aspirin, so she'll sleep most of the morning. Just fix her some soup a little later on. You're my right hand, Sylvie." Her mother kissed her on the forehead and hurried out the door.

Sylvia sighed with resignation. *Well, there goes my perfect attendance award! Just when classes are starting and I don't want to miss one single thing.* She fixed herself a bowl of oatmeal and settled down in front of the television to see what was happening at Central.

The doorbell rang just as the news crews were beginning to broadcast. Sylvia was surprised to see Aunt Bessie.

"Your mother called and told me DJ was sick."

"She made me stay home with her," Sylvia replied grumpily. "If I had known you were coming, I coulda gone to school."

"Well, your mother knows I never close the shop, but nobody is gonna be coming in to get their hair done today. It's not safe to be on the streets of Little Rock. I came to see if you needed a little company." She sat down on the sofa with Sylvia and they watched the news reports.

"That's an awfully big crowd of white people standing outside the school," Sylvia said. "They look pretty angry."

"Don't these folks have jobs?" Aunt Bessie asked. "They look like they're just waiting."

"For what?" Sylvia moved closer to her aunt. *I'm glad Aunt Bessie is here with me.*

"For something to happen. For the colored kids to dare to show up," Bessie replied ominously.

Sylvia watched the scene intently. "The white kids seem to be going in the building with no problem."

"Oh, look! The crowd is moving! What's happening? It's

like a giant white beast—moving in to attack. It's one of the colored kids. Poor baby. "

"It's Elizabeth Eckford!" Sylvia exclaimed. "She's all alone. Where are the other eight?"

She walked alone. Down that long sidewalk in front of the school, up to the steps that led to the front door, she walked with her head held high, slowly, deliberately. Dressed neatly in a white dress with black trim, she walked, looking neither to the right nor the left. She wore dark sunglasses.

"Lord, help her!" Aunt Bessie whispered.

"Why is she all by herself?" Sylvia watched—fascinated and horrified.

"She's getting close to the door!"

"There's some white kids in front of her—they're going in with no problem—the guardsmen are letting them by. She's gonna be okay." Sylvia rose to her feet.

"They're crossing their guns! I don't believe this! They're not going to let the child get past them!" Aunt Bessie was screaming at the television screen. "I thought the guards were there to protect the Negro kids!"

It was clear Elizabeth was frustrated—she tried several times to get past the guards. The last time she tried, they pointed their bayonets at her.

"They're pointing guns at her! Are they going to shoot a teenager on live television?"

"Oh, my Lord," Aunt Bessie mumbled, her eyes fixed on the television screen.

Sylvia grabbed her aunt's hand. "If that was me, I'd be so scared I'd be wetting my pants. I know she's terrified!"

Elizabeth turned then, glanced around to see what she

should do, or to look for help perhaps, and all that stood in front of her was a sea of angry white faces. She walked slowly down the steps, and as she got closer to what was now a mob, they grew fierce.

Sylvia started to cry as she watched. "Oh, Aunt Bessie, a lady is spitting on her."

"She's all alone," Aunt Bessie moaned.

"They're calling her names! How can grown-ups do that to a kid?" Tears streamed down Sylvia's face.

Elizabeth walked slowly and silently. It was unbelievable.

"Get her! Lynch her!" Aunt Bessie repeated the words in whispered disbelief as she heard them on the screen. "Get a rope and drag her over to this tree. Let's take care of this nigger now!" She gulped and looked at Sylvia. "How can this be happening?"

The faces of the people in the mob were distorted with hatred. Through it all, Elizabeth said nothing, but walked slowly toward the bus stop across the street.

"Aunt Bessie, she's trembling. She can't stop shaking. Won't somebody help her, please?"

The cameras kept losing her in the crowd, but Sylvia could see Elizabeth had finally made it to the bus stop. The mob jeered and cursed.

"Oh, look, somebody is going to help! One sane person in a sea of crazy people!" A white woman approached Elizabeth, sat down next to her at the bus stop, and put her arm around her. When the bus arrived, she helped her get safely into a seat.

As the smoke from the bus exhaust filled the air, the cameras were left to film only the filth and nastiness left behind. Sylvia ran to the bathroom and threw up.

Thursday, September 5, 1957
It turns out the other eight students showed up at another door of Central High yesterday. They were turned away and asked to leave. Elizabeth, who had not received the message about when and where to meet yesterday, had arrived at the school building without the others, which left her unprotected and at the mercy of the mob.

Her picture is on the front page of today's paper—probably every paper in America, Gary says.

People from the neighborhood have been in and out of the house all day, offering advice or encouragement or opinions. No one, not even me, seems to have talked to any of the Nine, as they are now being called. They are not answering phone calls or coming to the door. The entire colored community is upset. Some think we ought to quit and not try anymore, while others want to rush out and fight all white people. I've been trembling and nauseous all day. I keep thinking about Elizabeth, praying for her, understanding only a tiny portion of her pain. If I had been in her place, I don't think I could have been so brave. I *know* I couldn't have.

It's quiet at Central today, I heard. None of the nine will be going to school anywhere today. I wonder how they feel.

Friday, September 13, 1957
Today is Friday the thirteenth. The old folks says it's a day of bad luck, but I don't see how much worse it can get here. All the kids I

know are going to school in Little Rock except for the nine Negro students who want to go to Central High. They sit in limbo—waiting for a
decision, for safety. Everybody has an opinion, although only white opinions are printed in the newspaper. There's all kind of political stuff going
on, some of which I don't understand. The governor huffs and puffs and
makes public statements about how proud he is to be from Arkansas and
how he's not going to let the president tell him what to do. Judges are
saying integration must happen. Politicians are saying it will not.

Good old Governor Faubus went on television again tonight. He's
demanding that the federal government halt its demand for integration.
Can a governor do that? I thought everybody had to obey the president.

The reporter said that, because of a court order, Governor Faubus
had removed the National Guard from in front of Central and replaced
them with the Little Rock police. After guns and helmets and bayonets,
he's using our little police force? I stared at the TV screen in disbelief.

Has the governor *seen* our cops? They're fine with one or two
robbers or burglars, I'm sure. But a mob?

MONDAY, SEPTEMBER 23, 1957

Today's the day, Sylvie. They're going in, and I'm going to
watch it happen. You want to go with me?" Gary asked,
his voice a challenge. They stood in front of Mann High School,
waiting for the bell to ring.

"You want me to skip school?" Sylvia asked him incredulously.

"You scared?"

"Mama will kill me!"

"So stay here and watch it on the evening news. I'm leaving now. See you at home." He started to walk away.

"Wait, Gary." Sylvia had never done anything like this in her life. But maybe it was time to grow up. *I'm going!* "Let's go!" Sylvia said. She didn't look back as they hurried down the street.

Crowds of white people roamed the streets, aimlessly throwing rocks and bottles at homes in the colored neighborhoods. Most of the houses there had their curtains drawn. Gary led Sylvia carefully around the crowds and headed to the home of Daisy Bates. She gave Sylvia a big hug and did not seem surprised to see her. The nine students were sitting in two cars in front of her house. They did not wave.

"I'm getting ready to drive them to the school. There's a carload of Negro reporters with us. You two want to come?"

Sylvia nodded enthusiastically.

"You can ride with the reporters." Miss Daisy hurried down her steps.

As they got close to Central High School, Sylvia saw what seemed to be thousands of angry white people in front of the school, getting more riled up by the minute. Even the air, Sylvia sensed, seemed dry like timber—ready to burst into flame from any spark. Terrified, heart trembling, Sylvia pressed her forehead against the coolness of the car window, watching the hysteria build.

The driver parked and the reporters, cameras and notepads in hand, hopped out. Sylvia and Gary stayed in the car. In front of the school this time, instead of National Guardsmen, were local Little Rock police.

"Those cops look really scared," Sylvia whispered, her voice echoing the looks on their faces.

"They've got reason to be. That crowd could stomp them if they wanted to."

"Look!" Sylvia exclaimed. "They're getting in the side door! Finally!" She watched as the nine students, Elizabeth not by herself this time, scurried through the side door, police officers flanking them.

But someone in the crowd spotted them as they entered, and yelled, "They're in! The niggers are in!"

"Gary! They're going to mob the door!" Sylvia cringed.

Then the crowd moved as one being in the direction of that door. Sylvia could hear white mothers yelling to their children, "Come out! Don't stay in there with those niggers! Come out of there rather than breathe their air!"

"Are any kids coming out?" Sylvia asked. She had huddled down.

"Only a few. Looks like they're just looking for a new way to skip class." Then Gary cried out, "Sylvia! They're attacking the colored reporters with rocks and bricks! Open the door! Here they come!"

This car is no protection against a mob. Suppose they attack us? Sylvia envisioned herself being bandaged on her mother's sofa this time.

Heads bloodied and cameras broken, two of the reporters ran back to the safety of the car, where Gary and Sylvia crouched low in the backseat. "Are you okay?" Sylvia asked quietly. Blood trickled onto the car seat.

"We're fine," one of the reporters said breathlessly, "but we don't know about the Nine." Sylvia wasn't sure when everybody started referring to them as "the Nine" but the name seemed to have stuck.

"The mob is rushing the police barricades!" Gary said.

Sylvia could hear the people screaming, "Get the niggers out of there! Let's go get our shotguns!" She gasped.

"Are they going to be okay, Gary?"

"I see Miss Daisy's car moving around back. They're bringing the Nine out the back door. I guess we'll try again tomorrow."

"What happens now?" Sylvia asked as a car roared down the street, horn blaring.

"Two, Four, Six, Eight . . . We ain't gonna integrate!" The chant could be heard clearly, even though the car was far down the street. Another car roared by, full of teenagers, shouting loudly and forcefully, over and over until their voices faded. "Two, Four, Six, Eight . . . We ain't gonna integrate!"

As they drove away, Sylvia shuddered, gulping away tears.

Tuesday, September 24, 1957

Mama had a full-grown purple cow when she found out what me and Gary had done, but it was more because she was scared for our safety, instead of the fact we had skipped school. DJ looked up at me like I was a warrior queen or something—to buck Mama's rules and live is a pretty big deal. I didn't tell her I was so scared I almost wet my pants. Warrior queens don't do that.

Nobody went to school today. Not even those of us who go to the Negro schools. Parents are afraid to let their children out of their sight.

The mayor of Little Rock doesn't know what to do. I heard on the news this morning that he's asked President Eisenhower to send troops. Real soldiers, the kind that fight wars in foreign countries. The president called the rioting "disgraceful" and has ordered the army into Little Rock. They're supposed to be here by tonight. How did this happen to us?

The editor of the *Arkansas Gazette* stared bluntly at the TV camera last night and stated, "I'll give it to you in one sentence. The police have been routed, the mob is in the streets, and we're close to a reign of terror."

Around six this evening, I heard the roaring drone of airplanes in the distance. I peeked outside, and the sky was dotted with huge, dull green helicopters, throbbing against the shadows which had been clouds, and above them, dark green airplanes. I could hear sirens in the distance. It was like we were being invaded.

WEDNESDAY, SEPTEMBER 25, 1957—MORNING

Well, they're here, Mama. The soldiers are here," Sylvia said. Pictures of soldiers and tanks dominated the front page of the newspaper.

Mr. Patterson read out loud, "Twelve hundred members of the 1st Airborne Battle Group, 327th Infantry, 101st Airborne Division—paper says they're called the Screaming Eagles—are in our city and surrounding Central High School."

"Wow," Gary said.

"Are those soldiers good guys or bad guys?" DJ asked.

"They're from the President of the United States," Mrs.

Patterson explained. "They are here to make sure the law is enforced."

"And the law says the Nine can go to Central High?" DJ continued.

"Yep. That's been the problem from the beginning. Now they can," Sylvia explained.

No one had gone to school. The family huddled around the television set.

At 9:22 A.M. Sylvia watched proudly, with tears in her eyes, as the nine students entered the front door of Central High School. Not the back door. Not the side door. The front door like everybody else. Well, not exactly like everybody else. Twenty-two soldiers surrounded them. Helicopters circled above the school. Paratroopers stood on guard. The crowd had melted to just a few angry hotheads. The Nine were in.

TUESDAY, OCTOBER 1, 1957

Sylvia went to the phone, picked up the receiver, and started to dial. As she put her fingertips into the little white circles, she could hear the distinctive *zip, zip, zip* of the telephone dial as it spun around.

"Hi, Rachel. It seems like forever since I've talked to you. How's your mom and dad?" Sylvia twirled the phone cord in her fingers.

"So much better now that the rebuilding has started. Papa wakes up early every morning—making plans for the day instead of sleeping all day and refusing to get out of the bed in

Uncle Ruben's guest room. Uncle Ruben was about to kick him to the side of the road! And Mother is cooking again, so that's a good sign."

"What about you?" Sylvia asked. "It must be rough living with relatives."

"Tell me about it. Instead of a pretty new dress for the first day of school, I had to wear one of my cousin Hilda's old outfits. She's taller and skinnier than me, so I looked like the Wicked Witch of the West!" She giggled.

"I thought you looked pretty good," Sylvia said. "I saw you on TV."

"You saw that? Hmmph! Stupid reporters and their dumb questions!"

"I think you said just the right thing, Rachel, something the world needed to hear," Sylvia said honestly.

Ignoring the compliment, Rachel replied, "Did you see that cute boy who talked to me right after that?"

"No, they switched the camera to somebody who would say something mean."

"Well, there are plenty of those, and not as many cute boys as I thought there would be, so I still don't have a boyfriend yet." She paused. "School is crazy, Sylvia. Unbelievable."

"It's gotta be. So, tell me how it is—really. It must be really something behind those big old doors when the TV cameras aren't lurking."

"You want to know the truth? It's awful, Sylvia. Bomb threats are called into the school every day. We have to leave the building while they search for nothing."

"The protesters are just trying to disrupt the normal flow of things."

"Well, they're doing a pretty good job! You know, I think if they just left us alone, the kids would be fine. It's the grown-ups who are protesting and acting like idiots. They're the ones who are making it impossible for anybody to have a normal school day."

"Yeah, there's not a whole lot of normal going on in Little Rock these days," Sylvia said in agreement. "Crosses have been burned in front of some of the homes of the Nine."

"I heard. How horrible to wake up in the middle of the night with a Klan cross in your yard."

"About like waking up to find a swastika on your door. You've been there. Pretty awful."

"I think the only reason we haven't had another Nazi sign painted on our door is that we have no door!" Rachel said with a rueful laugh. "Papa's been pretty outspoken about how stupid the segregationists are—lots of people don't like that."

"Yeah, but isn't it cool the way folks are coming together to help your family and Miss Lillie to rebuild?"

"You're right. It makes it easier to deal with the rest of the craziness. Colored men are hammering in our building and white men are nailing stuff on Miss Lillie's side. Women of all colors making food for everybody. It's like a place where you can find water in the middle of a desert."

"I think my mother is sending over red beans and rice this week. She's sending better food over there than we're getting at home!"

"Tell DJ I have the latest Archie comic book. I've been saving them for her."

"Thanks." Sylvia paused. "Rachel, do you have any classes with any of the Nine?"

"A couple. I go out of my way to make sure nobody messes with them, but basically, I try to treat them like I'd treat anybody who needed to borrow a pencil or wanted to know what page the teacher was talking about. You know, like it's no big deal."

"They probably appreciate that. I think that's what I'd miss the most—everything being routine and ordinary. They never have a normal day, so it really is a big deal."

"Yeah, and then our bigmouthed governor gets on TV every night and makes sure everybody thinks the world is about to blow up," Rachel said, clearly annoyed.

"Last week I heard him say, 'We are now an occupied territory. Evidence of the naked force of the federal government is clear, in these unsheathed bayonets in the backs of schoolgirls.' Good grief!"

"What can you do when your leaders are nutso?" Rachel asked.

"Go to a school dance!" Sylvia replied with a laugh. "We've got the Halloween dance coming up soon."

"Folks at Central are scared to even schedule a dance. Trouble might show up," Rachel said grumpily.

"Speaking of trouble, I got a letter from Reggie a couple of days ago," Sylvia said, trying to keep the softness out of her voice.

"You know, he's been sending Papa seven dollars every single week."

"Yeah, he told me. He sends money to Miss Lillie, too."

"He's a good kid, Sylvie. Just confused. My parents have forgiven him and moved on. Daddy said life is too short to hold on to hatred."

"Your dad is something else," Sylvia said with real admiration.

"Hey, Sylvia, are you glad you're not one of the Nine, or sorry you're missing your chance to be famous, sort of?"

"I'm still gonna be famous. This just wasn't the time for me to be on the six o'clock news. But you just wait. One day, millions of people will know my name."

"I don't think anybody will remember me in a hundred years," Rachel said. "Actually, I don't think I'd want that. But I'd hope that you'd remember me."

"Always."

"Forever."

Monday, October 14, 1957

Today was a beautiful fall day. I walked home slowly, amazed at the colors of the leaves and softness of the breeze. It didn't seem like there could possibly be any turmoil anyplace where the weather was so lovely. But just a few blocks away, trouble still rumbles.

The problems at Central High won't be going away in a couple of days or weeks. It's going to be awful for the rest of the school year. Politicians and grown-ups are going to make it painful and keep picking at the sores they've caused all year. I think if the whole mess was left up to teenagers, we'd get through it just fine. If Little Richard and Jerry Lee Lewis can sing together on *American Bandstand*, it seems to me that folks in Little Rock ought to be able to go to school together. But nobody cares what I think—I'm no longer on anybody's list.

I don't feel guilty anymore that I'm not one of the Nine. It was not meant to be. They have sealed their place in history, and what I may be able to offer the world is still a mystery. I can live with that.

I pray that one day I may be able to make my way proudly with the courage and dignity of the nine students who are undergoing such abuse every day. There is no telling what the rest of the school year will bring, but I feel pretty good about the future. I'm ready for the fire next time it comes my way.

CHILDREN OF COLOR

We stand together
All of the
> full-toned
> dusk-hued
> dawn-tinted
>> children of the world

We're a colorful collaboration—
> fiery red
> deep mahogany
> goldenrod

Are we individuals
> like the tawny colors in a crayon box?
>> Burnt sienna
>> Auburn
>> Honey rose

Or are we blended
> like discarded watercolors in a glass?
>> Burned coffee

Muddy splashes
Melted caramel
    Washed together
    into one obedient dirty brown hue

We, the children of color—
    A combustible volcano
        Erupt in painted tones of terra-cotta
        black sweet anthems of blue
        honey-bright sunrise songs
            a chorus of copper symphonies—

We scream with dark intensity—
We shout with golden rage—

Let our voices be heard
Let out faces be seen
Let us shine.

Author's Note

IN THE NEXT FEW MONTHS, Little Rock, Arkansas, saw angry demonstrations as well as weekly prayer services for peace. The nine students bravely went to school each day, undergoing all kinds of abuse in the halls of Central High School. They had food thrown on them, acid thrown on their clothes, their lockers were vandalized, and their books stolen. They were pushed down steps, bullied in the halls, and called horrible names—every single day. Through it all, they endured. The governor and the politicians encouraged those who persecuted the nine students at Central High School. He tried actively, but unsuccessfully, all year long, to have the Nine removed. Few of the students who tormented the Nine were ever prosecuted for their actions.

The federal troops were gradually withdrawn as the school year progressed, and National Guardsmen, under the authority of the President of the United States, were assigned to protect the Nine inside the school. But they could not be inside classrooms or bathrooms or gym locker rooms, where much of the abuse took place. Eventually, the National Guardsmen were also removed, although the torture and persecution never ceased.

In December 1957, Minnijean Brown was suspended from school for spilling chili on two white students who had been harassing her. "One down and eight to go" was the chant heard in the halls. Minnijean was finally expelled in February 1958 for fighting back. She moved out of Little Rock.

As the early part of 1958 progressed, tensions mounted, and the harassment of the Nine increased. "Open Season on Coons" was typed on cards that were distributed at Central.

In spite of it all, Ernest Green became the first black student to graduate from Central High on May 25, 1958. He was told not to show up, threatened with violence if he participated in the ceremonies, but he joined six hundred other seniors to graduate. Federal troops and city police were on hand but the event went off without incident.

In an interesting side note, Dr. Martin Luther King, Jr. attended the ceremony almost completely unnoticed.

In July 1958, Governor Faubus was elected to a third term. "I stand now, and always, in opposition to integration by force, and at bayonet point," he said. In August, he called a special session of the state legislature to pass a law allowing him to close public schools to avoid integration. On September 15, 1958, Governor Faubus ordered all of Little Rock's high schools closed. They stayed closed the entire school year of 1958–59. Those students, both black and white, who were unable to find an alternative lost one entire school year. After much political wrangling, the schools reopened in September 1959, all of them integrated. Governor Faubus finally gave up.

Sylvia Faye and her family are fictional, but the nine students who integrated the school are very real.

Selected List of Web sites on the subject

http://www.archives.gov/education/index.html

http://www.ardemgaz.com/prev/central/

http://www.arkansas.com/state-federal-parks/national-federal-parks/central-hs.asp

http://www.ark-ives.com/photo/gallery/central.asp

http://www.centralhigh57.org/

http://www.cr.nps.gov/nr/travel/civilrights/ak1.htm

http://www.encyclopediaofarkansas.net/encyclopedia/entry-detail.aspx?entryID=718

http://www.historylearningsite.co.uk/little_rock.htm

http://www.littlerock.about.com/cs/centralhigh/a/Integration.htm

http://www.littlerock.about.com/cs/centralhigh/a/littlerock9.htm

http://www.littlerock.about.com/cs/centralhigh/tp/aatpcentral.htm

http://www.louisianahistory.ourfamily.com/arkansas/littlerock9.html

http://www.ourdocuments.gov/doc.php?flash=true&doc=89&page=transcript

http://www.usnews.com/usnews/documents/docpages/document_page89.htm